Richard Rawcliffe, John Rawcliffe

Pebbles Fro' Ribbleside

Richard Rawcliffe, John Rawcliffe

Pebbles Fro' Ribbleside

ISBN/EAN: 9783337815936

Printed in Europe, USA, Canada, Australia, Japan

Cover: Foto ©Andreas Hilbeck / pixelio.de

More available books at **www.hansebooks.com**

Pebbles fro' Ribbleside

BY RICHARD AND JOHN RAWCLIFFE.

PART I.

RICHARD RAWCLIFFE'S POEMS.

" To die is landing on some peaceful shore,
Where billows never beat, nor tempests roar ;
Ere well we feel the friendly stroke, 'tis o'er."
—*Garth.*

Blackburn :
J. & G. TOULMIN, CORPORATION STREET.
1891.

CONTENTS.

PART I.

Introductory and Biographical Note.

BLACKBURN, it is safe to say, has produced more weavers of calico and of verse than any other town in the United Kingdom. Not that there is any relation between the two; but the fact is there nevertheless, and should be taken into account by the gentle South, when, as sometimes happens, it grows harsh in its criticism of "the Northern barbarian." This taste for verse-making is surely indicative of a delicate striving after higher and better things; and that it has not been in vain is shown by the high level of excellence which has been attained during the past twenty years by at least a dozen of these wooers of the Muses. To what are we to attribute this undoubted tendency? To a common inclination to follow in a track once made? Or is it "something in the air," and the scenery? It is not improbable that all three factors have operated as formative influences. Blackburn, rude, grimy, and smoke-smitten though it be, is certainly happily situated with regard to its surroundings. Within a mile from its busy centre the workman can gain heights from which he may catch "glimpses which will make him less forlorn " of moorland and mountain, and valley and plain.   There is grand old Pendle and Blease-dale Fells, with Clitheroe Castle—a rocky islet in a sea of verdure—and the broad pleasant valley of the Ribble leading the eye by many a smiling mead until it reaches Preston, and widens to the sea. •Need we wonder that such scenes have attuned the soul to harmony, and that the tender emotion which has been stirred has occasion-ally found fitting expression in song ?

The late Richard Rawcliffe whose poems (issued by his brother along with his own) have the first place in this volume, was an ardent lover of nature, and as a lover was a keen observer of her ever-varying moods.   He was born in Ribchester on the 19th November, 1839, and was a son of John and Martha Rawcliffe.   Like his parents, Richard was early taught to earn a scanty living as a hand-loom weaver, but the power-loom having gradually superseded the hand-loom, he removed to Blackburn in August, 1858, and in his nineteenth year became a weaver in a cotton mill.   In 1860 he married his first wife, Esther Robinson, who bore him three children ; and it was during this first stay in Blackburn that he found his way into the " Poet's Corner " of local and other journals, and became a member of the Blackburn Literary Club.   In 1864 he returned to Ribchester, having been offered the post of overlooker at Ribblesdale Mill.   Here for a short period he was truly happy.   He had made a step in advance ; he was in his native village amongst people who knew him and liked him, and, as he himself expressed it, he was—

Away from smoke, to where the breezes free
Do kiss the flowery mead and craggy steep.

But death stepped in and snatched the cup from his lips ; ·
his wife died in November, 1865 ; and soon afterwards
he returned to Blackburn, to take a post as overlooker
at Peel Mill, which he held for five or six years. It was
whilst working here that he married again. The maiden
name of his second wife was Alice Formby, and she bore ·
him five children. He was afterwards employed in a
responsible position at Moorgate Mill ; and became Presi-
dent of the Blackburn Overlookers' Association. The
death of one of his sons from consumption was a great
blow to him. Whether his constant nursing of the sick
lad resulted in infection, or whether it simply developed
seeds within of the dread malady must ever be a matter
of conjecture. But it was not long after the death of his
son that it was seen that he, too, was stricken. He bore
up bravely, and kept at work as long as he could. But
the time came when he was unequal to the daily task,
and, with his savings melting away, the prospect before
him was indeed a dreary one. Still, he rallied occasionally ;
and like other consumptives he was ever hopeful of a
favourable turn. He was advised at length that the only
chance for him was to go to Australia. He had relatives
living in the country awide of Melbourne ; but, as his
means were exhausted, a number of his friends and well-
wishers subscribed something more than was sufficient
for the voyage out. The experiment was however made
too late. He left England for Australia by the "Garonne"
(Orient Line), on the first of September, 1886, and arrived
at Melbourne on the 16th October, reaching his new

home early next morning.   He was warmly received by
his relatives; and wrote a glowing description of his
surroundings ; the scenery, the constant sunshine and
the wealth of fruit and flowers being like a new birth to
him.   He was still hopeful, and yet the end was near.
He had preserved a descriptive record of the journey out
which he had promised to send me for publication.   That
record reached me ; it was a bulky letter ; I opened it
with a glow of pleasure, but what a shock I received !   A
brief note accompanied the diary.   It was in an unfamiliar
hand, and it announced that " Dick " had died somewhat
suddenly on the night of the 11th December, in the same
year, 1886.   He had sat up somewhat later than usual to
finish his writing.   Soon after he retired, he had a severe
fit of coughing, which was followed by hemorrhage of the
lungs.   The " fell sergeant, Death," had summoned him ;
and, before daylight, he had obeyed the summons and
was gone.

It would be out of place to make more than a brief
mention of John Rawcliffe, seeing that this book is
issued by him as a tribute, in some measure, to the
memory of his brother ; but it may be fittingly stated
that he was born in Ribchester on the 10th of February,
1844.   He left his native dale in 1858, about a fortnight
after his brother, having as a boy been bobbin-winder,
and then hand-loom weaver.   He went to Blackburn to
become a power-loom weaver; and was married to
Eleanor Hindle, his present wife, in 1867.   Singular·to
state, his first essay in verse was made whilst suffering
from a tumour in 1888—when he was forty-four years of

age. It is a literal, if somewhat grotesque, illustration of Shelley's saying that—

> Most wretched men
> Are cradled into poetry by wrong ;
> They learn in *suffering* what they teach in song.

The portrait of him, which is given in the volume, is in every respect satisfactory.

The portrait of Richard Rawcliffe, which prefaces his poems, scarcely does him justice. It is reproduced from a photograph taken when the effects of consumption were beginning to show themselves. The features are somewhat too angular, and the expression is lacking in that repose which was ordinarily characteristic of him. There was nothing pretentious about him—quite the reverse ; yet his bearing and manner were dignified and manly. Beneath an unassuming aspect, there was confidence in himself, and marked firmness of character. It went ill, as a rule, with anyone who tried a game of bluff with him. He had a quick eye for weak points, and his cool sarcastic shafts went straight to the mark. Although not possessed of what is termed the " gift o'th' gab," he was exceedingly ready at what Lancashire people call "bullocking ;" and he knew when it was fair to begin and when it was merciful to stop. His brother John had much less confidence in himself; and this striking difference in the brothers is seen in the fact that, while Richard took to poetising before he was out of his teens, it is only within the past few years—since, in fact, his brother's death—that John has discovered that he is possessed of a faculty for expression in verse. That he has worked the vein freely since he struck it is obvious

from the contents of this volume. He is not lacking in
genuine humour and artful simplicity ; but, as he would
be the first to acknowledge, while he is at home in the
dialect, he is not, like his brother, graceful and free in
ordinary English.   Richard Rawcliffe's poem, "Idyls by
the Hearth," though not free from minor defects, is fit
to be classed amongst the most charming pieces of verse
in the English language.   Take, for instance, the
following stanza :—

> Blushingly the clover glanceth
> Upwards, saying, "Can'st thou love me,
> Beauteous butterfly that danceth
>   Up above me ?"
> Then the butterfly alighteth,
> At these love-words spoke in bliss,
> And the clover he requiteth
>   With a kiss !

How playful and innocent the fancy, and how felici-
tously expressed !   And so all through.   The "Idyls"
are really the recollections of a factory worker in the
town of the sweet sights and sounds of his early life in
the country.   They are pebbles from the Ribbleside
which have been brilliantly polished and set as gems.

Richard Rawcliffe was fond of birds, and especially
of the Robin.   How suggestive of his own hard lot are
the lines in the first epistle to the Robin :—

> And when the sun has lost its glow ;
> And when thy spirit sinketh low,
> I love thee most, for then I know,
>   'Tis hard to sing, Red Robin.

The second poem on the same subject contains some
descriptive lines worthy to be preserved in memory,
such as :—

> While lush and strong, above the rill,
> Rears up the yellow daffodil !

Or—

> The thrifty bees, with constant hum,
> That tell us Summer time has come.

And—

> To hear again, through sunny rain,
>   The lively skylark sing ;
> So full of joy in heaven's blue,
> As if he knew not what to do.

There is nothing strained or far-fetched in anything that Richard Rawcliffe wrote. He "piped but as the linnets do "—that is to say he sang more to please himself and to express his feelings than with any thought of others, for he was free from the vanity of authorship. Perhaps it would have been better if he had had ambition in this direction ; for in that case his admirers would not have been left to regret that his poems are so few. But regret there is ; and that, after all, is the best compliment that could be paid to him as a writer.

                                    JOHN WALKER.

Warrington, July, 1891.

PEBBLES FRO' RIBBLESIDE.

Idyls by the Hearth.

Another weary day had fled,—
The fire was burning low and red ;
T'was late, my Ruth and babes in bed,
    Were soundly sleeping.
Outside the door the wintry rain,
Came tapping at the window pane ;
When calmly, softly, to my brain,
    Sweet thoughts came creeping.

The mouser watched beside the hole ;
The cinders one by one did fall,
And darkly on the kitchen wall
    Were shadows flitting :
And many an old familiar face,
Among the cinders I did trace,
While I, in my accustomed place,
    In thought was sitting.

A

Now ope the gate of vision swings !
Gay fancy lendeth Past her wings,
Who bringeth me delightful things,
        From boyhood's hours ;
And lureth me to sylvan dells,
With music sweet as distant bells,
Where round me groweth pimpernels,—
        Sweet scarlet flowers.

Every flower in beauty bloometh –
Roses, woodbine, everywhere —
Shed a fragrance that perfumeth
        All the air !
And the sun in beauty flingeth,
Jewels on the violet's bed ;
And the lark its matin singeth,
        Overhead.

Blushingly the clover glanceth
Upwards, saying, " Canst thou love me,
Beauteous butterfly that danceth
        Up above me ?"
Then the butterfly alighteth,
At these love-words spoke in bliss,
And the clover he requiteth
        With a kiss !

Then he flyeth on and smileth
Like a reckless wanton rover,
And the other flowers beguileth
        Like the clover.

"Sing, oh sing to me, thou poet!"
Thus a rose to me did say,
"And the brooklet shall requite thee
With a tuneful roundelay,"
  And thus I sung
  While o'er me hung
The wild red rose that Summer's day :—

"Oh, thou art a beauteous flower,
 The fairest in the grove,
Or ever graced the bower
 Where I am wont to rove ;
And in the emerald bushes,
Where sweetly sing the thrushes,
Thou hang'st thy head and blushes,
  Sweet flower of love !"

Then the rose exhaled a perfume
 To requite me for my song,
And the brooklet help'd to cheer me,
 Singing as it went along ;
But as I 'mong the daises sat,
 Entranced with the applause
Of the humming bee, the butterfly,
 The brooklet, and the rose,
I suddenly awoke and found,
 Alas, the vision fled !
And my Ruth, forsooth, there standing
 With the candle o'er my head,
Most earnestly imploring me
 To betake myself to bed !

To My Youngest Son.

[The following pathetic lines, written by the late Mr. Richard Rawcliffe, having been found between the leaves of a book in Australia, where that gentleman died, are recently to hand, and, as the MS. bears date November, 1886, they are in all probability the last lines of poetry that he wrote, which fact, we have no doubt, will lend a melancholy interest to their perusal.]

Dear Richard, how I long to hear
Thy voice in this fair hemisphere ;
And long to look once more on thee !
Thy presence here I feel would be
To me a source of pure delight,
To guide thy conduct day or night ;
And, in this distant clime, a ray
To cheer me thro' my life's dull way.

This sunny land would yield thee flowers
And fruits ; and all thy youthful hours,
My unsophisticated boy,
Would pass in bliss without alloy.
But ah ! 'tis but an idle dream—
The orchards and the gardens teem
With fruits and flowers, but then the sea
Too far divides us ; constantly
I see the waves lash into foam,—
Hear old familiar words from home,
With voices and unwilling sighs ;
'Tis then that tears spring to my eyes—
'Tis but a dream ! But come what may,
Improve thy mind, dear boy, each day,

And let thy every action shine
Among the good, while youth is thine ;
Then, wheresoever I may be,
I still, as now, will cling to thee.
What matters it how far I roam,
My heart, dear boy's, with thee and home !

Lines to a Poet Friend.

(REPLY TO "I AM THINKING, DEAREST,"
BY MR. JOHN WALKER.)

The music of thy song rings in mine ear,
   A pity 'tis that thou wert not more free—
Thou warbler with glad notes so loud and clear—
   That thou might'st sing and share my home with me.

Awhile ago and we were both together,
   Expecting not a change from youth to age ;
Exiled from verdant moorland, bush and heather,
   Like two lone vassal song birds in a cage.

And I would fain have borne with every ill,
   Excluded from the sun, content to pine
Away from Nature's ever-flowing rill,
   That I might every effort link with thine.

But duty led me, as a man asleep,
   Away from smoke, to where the breezes free
Do kiss the flowery mead and craggy steep,
   And thus my presence snatched away from thee.

I think oft-times of walks to Parlock hill—
   The purple ling that bloomed in beauty wild ;
And how the scene did us with rapture fill,
   Just as a flower with wonder fills a child.

While standing by the river's fitful side,
   The other day before the rains did fall,
A little robin-redbreast I espied
   Arising from the grass and sedges tall.

And straightway towards the hamlet it did fly,
   As if 't would say " King Winter, black and drear,
Approaches with his chilling breath, and I
   Unto some house must hie and seek for succour there."

And then I thought of many a wintry hour
   We two have passed with Shakspeare, Shelley, Moore,
And other bards who left the world a dower—
   Whose thoughts embodied are a constant store.

Oh ! that their hands did write in these our days—
   The truthful, fearless, and heroic band—
To make again the earth with wonder gaze,
   And nurse and strengthen freedom in the land.

Oh ! sing thee, poet, in thy cage of gloom,
   For thou art happy, though with toil confined,
More than a palace is thy humble room ;
   Thy brightest heaven is a stainless mind.

Sing on ! and let thy clear accented song
   Be oft repeated by the meanest slave,
Fight on ! and aim thy piercing darts at Wrong ;
   And if thou wounded art, thy wounds are brave.

Owð Blackin' Bill.

Id wur th' middle o' December an' th' northern wind
    dud blow,
A wake owd mon, hofe blind an' lame, went journeyin'
    i'th' snow ;
Id wor so cowd, his limbs did shake as he went up the
    hill.
"God love tho, lad," he sed to me,—he's code Owd
    Blackin' Bill.

"God love tho, lad ! ay t' same to thee ; God help tho
    on thy way,
An' gie tho strength that tha may poo throo th' moy-
    derins o' th' day."
An' then he went on limpin' wi' his basket reet up th'
    hill,
An' every child did run wi' joy to meet Owd Blackin'
    Bill.

Ah ! there never is a prattlin' child 'at plays i'th' village
    street
Bud runs to seeze his basket when they hear his trudging
    feet,
An' then he kindly gi's em bread an' cheese, wi' 'earty will,
'At fermers' wives i' charity have gi'n Owd Blackin' Bill.

Bud, eh ! one neet when id wur derk—there wornd a star
    i'th' sky,
Id 'ed bin rainin' durin' th' day, an' th' rooads wur nooan so
    dry—

Some reckless, drunken men wur coming past th' owd
    bobbin mill,
An' chanced to meet, an' by his feet, detect Owd Blackin'
    Bill.

One seized him roughly by the erm, another took away
His basket,—an' its contents wur his labours o' the day !
A long, long way he'd trudged that day—he'd bin past
Copstert Mill—
Yet into th' dam, o' side o' th' mill, they dipped Owd
    Blackin' Bill.

Id wurnd becose they spited him that they dud use him
    so,
An' if yo'll ax 'em wot 'twur for, they'll say us they durnd
    know,
An' even to this day they'll own as they regrettin' still
Th' unlucky neet as they did meet an' wrong Owd
    Blackin' Bill.

Oh ! oft, when bonny, tuneful birds their summer carols
    sing,
Owd Blackin' Bill limps on his way as happy as a king ;
He sits him deawn at th' foot o'th' wood, o' side o' th'
    ripplin' rill,
An' every bird i' th' wood 'll sing to cheer Owd Blackin'
    Bill.

There's nobry knows where he does live ; he's like a
    runnin' brook
At preedles on its way, an slyly peeps i' every nook ;

An' th' toper into th' aleheaws set invites him to a gill ;
"By gow," sez he, "aw am so fain to see Owd Blackin'
    Bill !"

Then meet him, rooasy childer, as he comes along the
    street—
Aw like to see an aged mon an' little childer greet ;
An' where aw wander into th' world, tho' friends may
    shun me still,
Aw's allus 'ev a kind regerd for poor Owd Blackin' Bill !

Summer.—A Lyric.

Leave the city's gloom and care,
For the morn is wondrous fair,
And the Summer with its mirth,
Gladdens all the face of earth.
Bound by no set form or rule,
Like a child released from school,
Shouts the cuckoo o'er the lea—
Shouting, shouting mellowly !

Far away from noisy mill,
Speedeth on the crystal rill,
By the foxglove and the rose,
Singing sweetly as it goes,—
Kiss'd by flower, and leaf and bud,
As it wanders thro' the wood—
As it journeys o'er the lea,
Singing, singing cheerily !

There's a freshness in the breeze,
Waving gracefully the trees ;
Here the burnished oak that shines ;
There the darkling group of pines :
Zephyrs o'er the fields of corn,
Steal the fragrance from the thorn,—
Waft the fragrance o'er the lea,
Wafting, wafting constantly !

Perching high on birchen bough,
That o'erlooks the busy plough,
On the hawthorn's snow-white bush,
Pipes the yellow-throated thrush,—
Flinging mirth mid Summer hours,
O'er the dell and thro' the bowers ;
Oh, its heart is full of glee,
Piping, piping merrily !

Lo ! the lark is mounting high,
Soaring upward to the sky,
With its bosom wet with dew,
Filled with joy in Heaven's blue,
And its psalm at Heaven's gate,
Makes me listen, watch and wait,—
Gladsome bird, so blythe and free,
Chanting, chanting holily !

how peaceful pat was mistaken for a fenian.

The morning was cold, for the frost it was keen,
And scarcely a soul in the street could be seen;
The sharp wind from the north without mercy did blow,
And the houses were white with the new-fallen snow.
The factories hummed with monotonous sound,
The milkman as usual was going his round,
When Paddy (excuse me for stating his name)
Whose toes with the pavement in contact they came,
With his coat without sleeves and his hat without crown,
Came along through the streets of our beautiful town.
Tho' his nose was quite blue with the frost that was keen,
Yet he hummed the sweet air of the shamrock so green;
Tho' his toes were but low, yet his spirits were high,
And you might have detected a joke in his eye!
He stopped at a pawnshop—the name I'll not mention—
To ransom some clothes with a part of his pension;
So he went to the door with a shout and a knock,
With, " Hello! D'ye know it is past eight o'clock?"
But no answer was made, and 'twas more than a joke
There to stand in the cold; so he took a short walk.
A policeman soon noticed the movements of Pat,—
He examined his shoes and he looked at his hat;—
He had studied the fellow—had formed his opinion,
And had not the least doubt he had dropped on a
    Fenian!
So he watched him, but kept out of sight in a lobby,
With his truncheon in hand, did that valiant bobby.
Now Paddy bethought him he'd rattle no more,
But would patiently wait till they opened the door;

So he leaned his long back 'gainst the door like a sentry,
When *Bobby springs on him* from out of the entry,
Saying, " What want you here—give me hold of your
    name,
Then make yourself scarce—I am up to your game !
You have no business here, with your back to the
    shutters."
But Pat soon retorts—mark the words that he utters :—
" Ye Englishmen boast of the laws of your nation,
But I do not admire them if, on this occasion,
You shove me from here,...but, bedad, I'll not go,
For this is my clothes-box, I'd have ye to know !"

To the Robin.

Of all the birds that sing and fly,
On tree-top or in azure sky,
Thro' smiles of Spring or Winter's sigh,
    I like thee most, Red Robin !

When Winter winds, across the moor,
Sweep by, and shake the cottage door ;
In frost and snow, unto the poor,
    Thou sing'st thy song, Red Robin !

And when the sun has lost its glow ;
And when thy spirit sinketh low,
I love thee most, for then I know,
    'Tis hard to sing, Red Robin !

And when it shines on wintry day,
And sends abroad its feeble ray,
It cheers me more than I can say,
  To hear thee sing, sweet Robin !

And when the pleasant voice of Spring
Is heard abroad, thou takest wing,
Among the choristers to sing,
  Thy pretty song, Red Robin !

By cottage door, or in the woods—
Among the fresh reviving buds,—
All thro' the year thy music floods
  Our little world, Red Robin !

On leafy branch or dewy spray,
Twittering gladly thro' the day ;
I would my lot were half so gay,
  And glad as thine, Red Robin !

— —

Money makes the Mare to go.

If you are wealthy, you are great,
 No matter what they say ;
And men of stamp on you will wait,
 If you've the gold to pay ;
'Twill raise you up, however low,
For " Money makes the mare to go."

"Gold is the root of evil," so,
  Some moralists will teach,
We might believe them, but we know
  For gold they write and preach.
Will they refuse the "root"? O, no,
For "Money makes the mare to go."

If you are poor, alas! you'll find
  That you must humble be;
You walk a step or two behind,
  And sometimes bend the knee
To those who have the gold; and so
'Tis "Money makes the mare to go."

What sullies many an angel face?
  'Tis abject poverty;
And brings to woman sad disgrace
  And, everlastingly,
Doth sink her more than we can know,
For "Money makes the mare to go."

What fills our workhouses and jails?
  What vice and misery spreads,
And every good intent assails—
  On each good action treads?
'Tis poverty, for well we know
That "Money makes the mare to go."

Refining learning you may gain,
  And things for aye untold;
For you may buy another's *brain*
  If you have got the gold.

'Twill shield you safe from every foe
For " Money makes the mare to go."

Be honest in whate'er you do,
    While young, or when you're old,
Get learning and refinement too,
    But don't forget the gold—
It is the soil where both will grow
For " Money makes the mare to go."

The Birds are Singing.

The birds are singing in the woods,
    The primrose from its bed is peeping ;
Adown the wold the crocus buds ;
    Around our house the ivy's creeping ;
The cowslips bloom upon the lea,
    Yet I am sad, bereft of thee.

'Tis not the singing birds or flowers
    Afford this heart of mine relief ;
The music from the woodland bowers
    Comes but to add unto my grief ;
The lapwing moans unceasingly,
    Or loudly chants thy obsequy.

O, would I were a little flower,
    A wild wood-rose, a light bluebell,
That I could smile amid the shower,
    No cheerless heart, no grief to tell ;
And I would bloom and flourish free
    Without a sense to feel for thee !

Our little boy of five years old,
   With rosy cheeks and azure eyes,
To me his simple tale he told
   Of happiness beyond the skies ;
He told me God had taken thee
   To make a home for him and me.

The birds are singing in the woods,
   The primrose from its bed is peeping;
Adown the wolds the crocus buds ;
   Around our house the ivy's creeping ;
The cowslips bloometh on the lea,
   Yet I am sad, bereft of thee.

Lines on the Death of Councillor Beads, J.P.

One more to the majority hath gone,
This one a leader of the many,—one
Who took his share in great affairs of state,
And loved the working-class to elevate.

For to that order he belonged.   His pride,
Thro' all their strivings, was to be their guide;
He worked unceasingly with pen and tongue,
And battled for the weak against the strong.

In politics was sound unto the core,
And for the truth he many an insult bore.
What cared he ?   He was affable and kind
To all, nor leaves an enemy behind !

He trod the footprints of the saints, and taught
The doctrines of the One whose grace he sought;
With wondrous power and with fervour preached,
And thus the hearts of those who heard were reached.

He soared above all parties, and our town
Owns not a man of more deserved renown,
For who could half defend its rights so well?
Let those he leaves behind, and history tell!

Toll the slow bell and lower the flags half-mast,
The soul of a true patriot has passed
Away! Tears shed! For he will weep who reads,
In type of mourning, of the death of Beads!

May Song.

The storm is hushed to-day,
Sleeping in the lap of May;
And yet there's strife and tumult in the town;
Then come, O, come away,
Enjoy the charms of May,
For the Robin to the woodland wild hath flown.

Let's go at early morn,
Where the tender blades of corn,
Rejoicing in their soil congenial seem;
And hear the merry thrush,
Sing above the verdant bush,
A song inspired by morning's golden beam!

O, come along with me,
Where the zephyrs moving free,
Steal the fragrance from the hawthorn as it blooms,
Let's go among the fields,
While Nature smiles and yields
Fairest landscapes that are breathing rich perfumes.

See the cowslips in their pride,
Blooming down the meadow side,
And the primrose of its parent sun's own hue ;
Lo, the lark is on the wing,
Blissful chorister of Spring,
Soaring upward with its bosom wet with dew !

The storm is hushed to-day,
In the downy lap of May ;
Alas ! there's strife and tumult in the town ;
Then come, O, come away,
Enjoy the charming May,
For the Robin to the woodland wilds hath flown !

In Blackburn Park.—To Flora.

Fair Flora ! Lovely goddess of the flowers,
Who holdeth sway thro' Spring and Summer hours,
Henceforth I hold myself thy devotee,
So hear my song, tho' much unworthy thee !

Scarcé had fell winter, tyrant among kings,
Swept from earth's lap all dear, delightful things—
Which made each song-bird mute, and every flow'r
Had perished 'neath his arrogative power,—
When lo ! Thou tripping cam'st and took thy stand,
Upon thy rocky throne ; and thy command,
Linked with thy modest form and witching grace,
Dethroned, and hurled the tyrant from his place !
Then every little shrub, and flower, and tree—
Etherial butterfly, and bird, and bee—
Came gladly forth—invited thee to stay,
And on thy forehead placed the crown of May !

———

Cherley Shepsterd.

Yo' see yon heawse a-top o' th' hill,
   Aside o' th' owd Stydd barn ;
An' deawn at th' bottom ther's a schoo',
   Wheer childer gooas to larn :
It's theer wheer Cherley Shepsterd lives,
   A chap wot's ne'er bin wed ;
He looks as if he wooar a mask,
   His nooas end bein' so red !

Yon little lad's moor sense than him
   Wot's trudgin' off to schoo' ;
He clams hissel to save his brass
   Then spends id like a foo' ;

He never weyves aboon a month
  Befoor he's toddlin deawn,
An' his iron'd clogs he swings away
  To Jooan's at t' " Rooas an' Creawn."

One Frida' he wer tekkin' up
  Fro' one of his drukken sprees ;
His lips wer white an' his nooas-end blue,
  An' th' wind rooar'd leawd i' th' trees :
Aw'd just popp'd in to see him
  An' he look'd i' sich a state,
I' th' midst o' cowd December,
  Wi' t' fire brunt deawn i' th' grate !

A hard owd mon is Cherley, too,
  He doesn'd dine o' treawt,
Or other bits o' niff-naffs
  Whol he brings hissel abeawt,
But weyves until he's hungry—
  He wants no feawl or fish—
An' maks as mony porritch then
  As fills a two-quert dish.

He doffs his cap and sits o' th' stoo',
  Wi' t' dish upon his knees—
That's when he's bravin' t' dismals
  Brought on wi' his drukken sprees—
An' if he corn'd quite sup 'em o',
  He darts ageon i' th' shop
To weyve until his bally yawns,
  Then sups 'em, every drop.

" Aw'll bring tha to 't, preawd stummick,"
　　Thus he mutters to hisself ;
As t' porritch dish, wi' t' porritch in,
　　He puts a-top o' th' shelf ;
Then weyves till th' loom an' t' shuttle sings,
　　An' his feet gooas up an' deawn,
But every piece as he poo's eawt
　　Is a stride to'rt t' " Rooas an' Creawn."

Bud, eh ! Th' owd lad is woss for wear
　　Aw met him t' other neet
Gooin' mopin' on up th' owd Stydd loyn—
　　He's welly lost his seet.
He wer mekkin' to'rt his lonely hooam
　　When fooak wer o' i' bed :
Aw could tell him bi his limpin' gait
　　An' his nooas end bein' so red.

———

In Memoriam.

SAMUEL PERRINGS, DIED JANUARY 9TH, 1877.

One of the tuneful tribe has gone to rest—
　　A bard whose verse was of the modest kind
Tho' fit to rank companion with the best—
　　To captivate and elevate the mind.

A cripple from his birth, and weak his frame,
　　His intellect was strong, his life was pure ;
And tho' in humble life he moved, his name
　　Among our sons of song shall aye endure.

Who hath not seen him in our streets around,
   Confin'd in a rude chair, and trailing on,
As full of energy as if the ground
   Was harass'd with the load that he put on !

And, if you hail'd him, he would give his hand—
   Tho' such a hand as was no hand, forsooth—
And greet you with a smile, serene and bland,
   That made you feel his honesty and truth.

And notes of modest beauty oft he flung,
   To multitudes who listen'd to his lay :
Of Grecian and of Servian slave he sung,—
   Such songs as cheer'd his simple, lonely way.

No pomp, or idle show attendant there,
   When mournfully his corpse was borne away ;
But audibly was heard full many a pray'r,
   When his frail form was lowered in the clay.

A genial, kind, and open-hearted friend
   From every care and toil hath found release ;
Who fought a hard fight bravely to the end,—
   May his departed spirit rest in peace !

Lines to the Robin.

Fly from thy shed, thou Robin Red,
   And sing thy pretty song ;
Near shady wood, and rear thy brood,
   Among the winged throng :
For nights and days are dark and drear,
And I am sad while thou art near.

Full oft I've fed thee, Robin Red,
   Throughout the wintry days ;
When winds blew keen—where thou hast been
   Beside my door always :
Now I would have thee far away,
So Robin Red no longer stay !

The crocus buds, and in the woods
   A stir of life is seen ;
Lo ! hedges bare, and everywhere,
   Freshens with shoots of green ;
While lush and strong, above the rill,
Rears up the yellow daffodil !

In shelter'd dells, and mossy cells,
   Beneath the hawthorn bush,
The woodbine creeps ; the primrose peeps,
   Up at the piping thrush,
Who sings a loud and measur'd note,
As if he'd bells within his throat !

I long to see the flow'ry lea,—
   The shooting of the corn !
To see again, in winding lane,
   The dew bespangled thorn—
The thrifty bees, with constant hum,
That tells us Summer time has come !

I long to hear hear the note so clear,
   Of cuckoo on the wing ;
To hear again, thro' sunny rain,

The lively skylark sing,
So full of joy in heaven's blue,
As if he knew not what to do !

When Autumn's fled, O, Robin Red,
    And flowers and leaves depart ;
Fly back to me, and thou wilt be
    The dearest to my heart ;
And with thy sweet and plaintive song,
Again we'll pass the winter long.

The Motherless Child.

A little one, laid by its mother's side,
    A lovely, artless child,
Ere she closed her weary eyes and died,
    Looked up in her face and smiled,
As if it would say, " Thou art going away,
And, mother, I do not wish to stay."

Ere fourteen years their course had run,
    One day in the springtide hours,
An angel did whisper, " Thy task is done !
    Come, lay down thy books and flowers ;
The dear ones, too, who have fostered thee
Must suffer thee now to depart with me."

'Twas then it gazed with vacant eyes
    On the few who were in the room,
That the angel did bear it away to the skies

A flower from the earth in full bloom !
Ah ! fondly it obeyed the mandate given
To dwell by the side of mother in heaven !

Ode to th' Canary.

Good lad thee, Dick, thy pratty wings
Vibrate wi' joy whene'er tha sings ;
Tha's bin a rare good bird to me,
Aw think its time aw sung for thee !

Hung up bi'th window in a cage,
Tha does thi best, although thi wage
Tha geds is watter and sum seed,
An' neaw an' then, sum garden weed.

If aw could mek tha understand,
Aw'd soon explain to thee heaw grand
Id is to keawr me in this cheer,
An', listen to thi songs up theer !

Sumtimes tha'rt singin' when aw'm sad,
As if tha meant to mek mo mad ;
Neaw Dick, aw think its owt but reight,
To sing when 't childer's pinched for meyt.

Poor, humble, an' contented bird,
Aw often think thi lot is hard ;
Thi heawse looks varra slim and poor,
An' there's no number on thi door.

Jack joiner med id, an' he said—
" Tha stood th' godfeyther for eawr Ned "—
It's bud a tooathri booards cut thin.
An' wired o' reawnd to keep tha in.

If theaw could think and talk thisel,
Tha'd hev some grievances to tell—
Sum strong accusements would ta find,
No deawt—if tha' could speak thi mind.

One neet, aw know, when aw looked up
At thi feawntain, ther wer nowt to sup ;
An' theer tha keawr'd just like a meawse,
An' nod a bit o' seed i' th' heawse !

Tha never geds i' sad disgrace,
Like theawsands do o' th' human race ;
An' clumsy mortals, sich as me,
Mut mony a lesson learn fro' thee.

Sing on, then, Dick ! Thy song o' glee
Hes scooars o' times delighted me ;
Aw'll keep thi drawer weel filled wi' seed,
An' gie tha bits o' garden weed !

In Memoriam.

JOHN RAWCLIFFE, born at Ribchester ; died at Padiham, July
31st, 1876 ; interred at Hurst Green Cemetery, August 3rd, aged 66.

A tribute to a father from a son,
Just when a toiling pilgrimage is done,
May be vain idleness, but this I know—
That he was worthy more than I can show.

A " life is but the journey of a day,"
An hour of fitful shade ; perchance a ray
Of sunshine then darts forth amid the gloom,
But Sorrow oft escorts us to the tomb.

How strange and how unkind seems death to those
Who watch a loved one sink to his repose !
Yet he was patient, and, with faithful trust
In Providence, shook off his mortal dust.

His faith in Christianity was true,
And all the names of Patron Saints he knew ;
Oft good examples in their lives would find,
And teach their precepts to the youthful mind.

In politics, was sound unto the core,
And, like an oak, he every tempest bore !
For, to the strong he never bowed the knee,
But sided with the weak for liberty.

Though in a humble sphere his lot was cast,
He bravely fought life's battle to the last ;
The wealthy who in loftier circles soar
Must thus submit—e'en they can do no more.

Of Nature he was fond, and, at the sound
Of warbling birds, the fields he lingered round ;
When woodland rose revealed its fairest blush,
He felt enraptured with the piping thrush.

Born in the hand-loom days, his eyes have seen
A change come o'er this fitful world, I ween—
Science advance and rural sports recede ;
And cares that were upon his brow we read.

A patient, persevering son of toil,
No foe he's left behind his name to soil.
He said " Good bye,—my life has run it's lease !"
We stood and gazed—his spirit fled in peace !

JOHN RAWCLIFFE.

Pebbles fro' Ribbleside

BY RICHARD AND JOHN RAWCLIFFE.

―――――――

PART II.

JOHN RAWCLIFFE'S POEMS.

―――――――

" Rude am I in speech,"
. . . .
" Little shall I grace my cause."
—*Shakespeare.*

PEBBLES FRO' RIBBLESIDE.

PART II.

An Apostrophe: To My Books.

Mi books, befoor to-morn's breet sun shall shine,
Yo'll be away; yo'll nod be books o' mine.
Like me, when aw wer young, yo'r turn'd adrift,
Among strange fooak i' different teawns to shift.
But O, as time draws near when we've to part
Strange feelin's come a-creepin' reawnd mi heart;
Ay, mony a happy heawr aw've hed wi' yo';
Far mooar than t'world 'll ever kear to know.
Bud, hevin' fun a place for every one,
Aw'll try mi best to bear id like a mon.
My brother scems to smile thro' mony a line
(An' when t' truth's towd aw'm preawd o' some o' mine!)
For t' weakest childer t' mooast affection's shown,
'Cause every gradely mother likes her own:
Bud durn'd ged preawd and think yorsel too grand
'To mate wi' moral books 'at's second-hand,—

Durn'd climb too high—yo'll nod hev far to fo',
For t' Robin sings his song on t' back-yard wo'!
Whol t' lark wi' lofty nooat sings sweet i' th' sky—
Yet t' robin may charm odd·'uns passin' by.
When t' speckled throstles pipes their silvery nooats
Ther's little twitterin' birds 'll tune ther throoats.
When t' moon's at full, an' shinin' clear an' breet
Some little twinklin' stars 'll come i' th' seet.
Be thankful when yo see books claim reneawn
As yo'r quite eawt o' t' reych o' envy's freawn!
Near th' owd Green-side, wheer Ribble wanders past,
An' wheer aw hooap they'll lay me deawn at last.
In after years aw may yet live to see
Yo' spreaded eawt on some fair woman's knee,
Wheer gradely fooak wi' gradely fooak con meet
Reawnd winter's fires wheer tales are towd at neet.

·   ·   ·   ·   ·   ·   ·   ·   ·   ·

In spring or in Summer-born June,
　　Fooak 'll wander abeawt into t' fields;
When t' birds are i' feather an' tune,
　　Or to pick nuts as Autumn-time yields;
But i' Winter, when t' neets are so long,
　　When hooam looks so cosy an' sweet,
Yo' may join in ther mirth an' ther song
　　Whol they're camping reawnd fire of a neet.

When owd Sol hes done o' his day's reawnd,
　　An' unbarr'd his gowd door into t' west;
An' when shadows cum creepin' o'er t' greawnd,
　　Fooak 'll mek tort ther hooams to find rest:

Then they may, just for t' sake of owd time,
    Mek yo' welcome when t' villagers meet,
An' may read fro' yo' some simple rhyme,.
    Whol they're campin' reawnd t' fire of a neet.

.   .   .   .

Neaw tho' yo'r gooin away to friends o' mine,
I' t' world o' books yo' cornd expect to shine,
They're sent away fro' t' printers neaw bi' t' looad,
Then thrutched i' nooks an' corners eawt o' t' rooad.
Ther's some o' yo' as may ged lent, or lost,
It's best, mi books, to be prepared for t' wost.
Yo' may ged crushed wi big an' nowty books,
Or left to fret or pine i' dusty nooks.

For weeks an' weeks whol some owd sluggard dame,
Is med to come an' cleyn, thro' fear or shame,
An' when hoo's been i' every other room,
Hoo may then come to yo', an' bring her broom,
An', mutterin' to hersell o'er dusty weather,
May tek an' shake an' jowl yo'r heyds together.
Hoo'll happen rub yo'r back and cleyn yo'r face,
An' put yo' reet to t' front i' t' nicest case.
I' t' life o' books strange things may come to pass,
Yo' may ged ta'en an' sowd for ready brass !

Excuse me, books ! Aw'm moved to tears,
Aw'm thinkin' o'er these auctioneers—
Like critics, they're i' every teawn—
They lift books up to knock 'em deawn !
To ged knock'd deawn because yo'r bowt,

An' ta'en away for t' next to nowt,
To some owd musty broker's shop,
Wheer theives an' rooags 'll often stop !
For, speykin neaw, 'tween yo' an' me—
Nod wod aw've heeard, bud wod aw see
(Durn'd turn id o'er when yo've bin towd—
Aw've watch'd 'em till mi blood's run cowd),
Aw've seen men bring a rooap an' string,
An' hoist books up to led 'em swing.
Aw've bidden whol aw couldn'd bide
To see books hung at's ne'er bin tried !
Bud cheer up, books ! an' hooap for t' best—
Yo' may yet find a haven of rest.
Aw know ther's mony an oppen hand
'Ll smile to greet yo' when yo' land.
They'll look to yo' when bent wi' age :
My brother's name's on mony a page ;
Aw hooap yo'll allus howd id fast,
An' keep it nice an' cleyn to th' last.
His every line wi' yo' aw'll trust,
Whol men an' books booath come to dust- -
Till death meks earthly singin' dull,
An' angels' songs moor beautiful !

Wben Everybody Geds their Own.

Aw dreamt last neet aw'd th' magic wand,
  An' th' lamp to see on every throne ;
An' things wer changed at my command,
  An' fooak could claim an' ged their own.
    Religious fooak hed o' agreed,
    Of every colour, every creed ;
    An' Avarce' poss hed bin untee'd,
  An' everybody geet their own.

An' sitch a change as wor i'th teawn,
  Wi' pen o' mine con ne'er be shown ;
For things seem'd flyin up and deawn,
  Bud everybody geet their own.
    Aw' see pianos, heeard um play,
    An' then they seemed to walk away
    Fro' fooak as never meant to pay,
  An' everybody geet their own.

Aw waved mi wand o'er t' pop-shop dooar,
  Then stown things fooak hed browt to pawn ;
Fro every shelf fell flop to t' flooar,
  An' everybody geet their own.
    An' t' fooak as hed th' mooast childer geet
    I'th biggest heawse i' every street ;
    An' rogues wer o' put eawt o'th seet,
  An' everybody geet their own.

An' then aw went to th' werkheawse gate,
  Aw'd heeard th' owd fooak gie mony a moan ;
Aw could'nd do to see um wait—
  They toddled reawnd an' claimed ther own.

                               c

In there they'd perted mon and wife,
  Aw waved mi wand an' banished strife ;
  Owd couples wer re-wed for life,
An' everybody geet their own.

An' every church i' th' land wer free,
  An' fooak flocked in when this wer known ;
An' th' rich wi' t' poor hed bent their knee,
  An' God's rich gifts wer o their own.
    An' saintly footprints show'd so plain,
    Men dud'nd preach for earthly gain ;
    For hope hed come an' banished pain,
  An' everybody geet their own.

For Truth hed come on t' earth to dwell,
  An' kicked eawt smiling flattering fawn ;
An' toll'd big supersticion's knell,
  An' everybody geet their own.
    For mony a place there wor abeawt,
    Where common sence wur livered eawt ;
    An' th' air wer rent wi' mony a sheawt,
  As everybody geet their own.

Owd Discooard kicked an' breathed his last,
  Then friendship spooak wi' sweeter tone ;
An' merit won i' every cast,
  An' everybody geet their own.
    For envy hed foo'n fast asleep,
    An' owd dull care wer buried deep ;
    Life's broo' worn'd hawf as rough an' steep,
  For everybody geet their own.

Aw think this life is bud a dreeam,
  An deeath u'll be like morning's dawn ;
When rogues no moore u'll plot an' skeeam,
  An what's bin stown u'll o be shown.
    Ut finish up o' life's short race,
    An' when we've doffed eawr rags an' lace,
    Then th' pooar may climb to th' topmost place,
  An' everybody ged their own.

———

3n Memoriam.

ELLENOR SHORROCK, died March 2nd, 1889, aged 4 years
and 6 months.

So full of life—now dead—in one short week ;
  'Twas better not to know the world's rude frown.
Where thou art I will ever try to seek—
  Thy brow is decked with God's immortal crown.

I wander now in Blackburn Park alone,
  The thrush's song can only give me pain,
The water rolls along with mournful tone—
  To Auntie's thou wilt never come again.

And I had hoped to lead thee by the hand,
  To show thee Spring in all her beauty drest,
Her bright robe trailing o'er the smiling land,—
  But thou didst haste to reach thy Father's rest.

The snowdrop's rising from the frozen ground,
 And soon the daises will bedeck the sod ; .
All these upon thy grave will soon be found,—
 Thou hast gone home : it was the will of God.

AN EPISTLE

To a Cousin Suffering from Cancer.

Be Patient, Lass, Do.

It's thi birthday to morn,
 Bud aw'm writin' to-day,
For time like a shadow
 Keeps flitting away.
Theaw'rt learning thy patience
 I' suffering's rough skoo ;
Just read on to th' finish,
 Be patient, lass, do.

This life's nod o' sunshine,
 We've sleet an' we've rain ;
For pleasures soon vanish
 An' leave us wi' pain.
Aw've kept slippin' back'ard,
 Theaw'rt welly up t' brow ;
Theaw'll land where it's breeter,
 Be patient, lass, do.

Theaw's booked thro' for heaven,
  Theaw's sin its breet ray,
But th' world an' its pleasures
  May leead me astray.
Aw corn'd show credentials
  Nor virtues enoo ;
Theaw'll werk eawt thy passage
  Be patient, lass, do.

An when theaw'rt in heaven
  Wod greetin's ther'll be.
Aw wish theaw could just speak
  A good word for me.
I' my heart, like mi head,
  Ther's a soft place or two ;
Aw wish aw could help tha,
  Be patient, lass, do.

Theaw'll then see eawr Nelly
  As never knew sin ;
Just tell her fro' me neaw
  Aw want to come in ;
Hoo'll ax' 'm so nicely,
  They'll led me go thro' ;
Aw's find tha wi' t' singers,
  Be patient, lass, do.

FEB. 13th, 1890.

Aw Wish Hoo'd Cum To-Neet.

My wife hoo's bin away o week,
  Eawr Tom's looked after t' shop ;
Aw think bi th' letter as hoo's sent
  Hoo's nod so long to stop.
Her letter's plain, it's just like hor,
  It's rather short an' sweet ;
Hoo ses ther is no place like hooam—
  Aw wish hoo'd cum to-neet.

It's terrible quare when hoo's at home—
  Hoo'll sauce mo mony a time ;
Hoo tells mo too aw'm fit for nowt
  Bud mekkin' silly rhyme.
An' neaw then, when hoo's far away,
  Hoo co's mo dear owd Jack,
An' ses hoo's my affectionate,
  An' wishes hoo were back.

Aw know hoo used to talk like thad
  At time we use to cooart ;
Bud sin thad weddin' knot wer teed,
  Ther's seldom owt o' th' sooart.
Hoo's hed an angel's visit neaw,
  An' med mi heart feel leet ;
Aw'll carry o her luggage hooam—
  Aw wish hoo'd cum to-neet.

Her cheer, like me, looks lonesum neaw,
  It's sulkin' into th' nooak ;

My pipe aw've nossed id day bi th' length,
    Aw've hed no heart to smook.
My collar button brasted off,
    An' when aw felt id crack,
Aw knew aw couldn'd set id on
    Because it's reet at back.

Eh ! what's thad pooastmon browt ageean ?
    A letter aw con see ;
Eh ! Tom, tha'rt fain to read id, lad,
    Bud nod as fain as me.
We's see her smilin' sunburnt face,
    Aw'll kuss id when we meet,
For t' letter ses " Just wait for me,
    Dear Jack, to-morn at neet."

———

Shy Little Miss.

She's a shy little miss,
    But she's fond of a kiss,
Though she's only eleven months old ;
    And when sleepy she'll cry,
    With a tear in each eye,
But she won't go to sleep when she's told.
    When awake you should see
    How she dances with glee,
While her cheeks get as red as a rose ;
    They may put on her hat
    When they take her a-tat
But she won't have them wiping her nose !

When dimpled her chin,
There is laughter within—
It is sunshine to me is her face ;
For when out of my room
There is nothing but gloom,
And the things always seem out of place.
Then I do feel so cross,
I'm afraid she is lost,
And my feelings I cannot compose ;
There's a cry I well know !
To the rescue I go,
When I find they are wiping her nose !

If she gives me her smile,
I am happy the while,
And I care not what selfish men say,
For this life is not long,
And the world's often wrong ;
Let the star of love shine on her way !
For I know when I'm sad,
She will cheer her old dad,
How she loves me there's nobody knows !
I can keep on good terms,
While I'm praising her charms,
But I can't when I'm wiping her nose !

I have care, I have strife,
In my struggle with life,
And grim Sorrow may come to my door ;

But well do I know
He will soon have to go,
When I hear a pit-pat on the floor,
For I know it's her feet—
How my heart it will beat !—
And myself I don't wish to disclose,
But so slyly she'll peep,
Then away she will leap—
She's afraid of me wiping her nose !

I have heard men who preach,
And I think they all teach,
That there's angels in heaven above ;
But I know, since her birth,
There is one upon earth,
And 'tis her that shall teach me to love !
She is bright, she is fair ;
Though she hasn't much hair,
I can patiently wait till it grows ;
She is handsome and stout,
She'd be happy without,
If they would not keep wiping her nose !

Old time is a thief
If we entertain grief,
But, like Nell, I can smile through a tear,
So I care not a jot,
For whatever's my lot,
I will never count life by the year.

But I trembled last night,
She'd a terrible fright,
So I tried and I found out the cause ;
She had waked in a dream—
Oh how hard she did scream !—
For she dreamt I was wiping her nose !

But she's naughty indeed,
For she knows she can't read,
Though sometimes she will earnestly look ;
And she thinks she's a right,
So she pulls with her might,
When I'm reading my paper or book.
Now I don't like to tell,
But her name it is Nell.
She is welcome wherever she goes,
Like the bright month of May ;
But then still I must say
She 'frigs' when they're wiping her nose !

AUG. 24th, 1889.

Phrenology.

Aw'm beawn to learn phrenology,
Aw've bowt t' book for t' job ;
It's nice to feel eawtside an know,
Whod fooak hes i' their knob.

Just look at me, I wed eawr Nell,
  An thout aw'd med a mark ;
An' neaw when thirty year's gon past,
  Aw find her yure's to dark !

It's strange aw never thowt o' this,
  An' bin deceived so oft ;
When fooak hes cum an' towd their tales,
  Aw've awlus bin so soft.
An' that's th' way as aw've getten wrong,
  Like,—never gradely shure ;
Aw'll feel ther heads, that's whod aw'll do,
  They'll nod cheat me no moore !

An' th' best on 't is, it's good to learn,
  Ther's th' index into th' book ;
Aw've nowt to do bud oppen th' page,
  To find um o' th' fost look.
An' every bump's so plainly mark'd,
  On th' model med o' pot ;
An' th' little squares wi' t' numbers on,
  As shows mo reet to th' spot.

Whey, bless mi life, ther's nowt so strange,
  At me bein' sitch a foo ;
They never learn't mo nowt like this,
  Whod bit aw went to t' skoo.
Aw've bin so fast when th' wife's bin crammed,
  An' sterted wi her din ;
Aw've nobbut fun id eawt this week,
  As th' temper's in her chin !

Last neet, aboon o' other neets,
   When sittin wi eawr Nell ;
Aw thowt id hardly reet to keep
   This knowledge to myself,—
Aw browt my books to find her t' place,
   An' show which bumps wer wrong ;
Aw prooved as hoo'd conbativeness,
   Bi th' way hoo used her tongue !

Aw see a bad case yesterday,
   When passin' Blinker's farm—
Aw see two cooarters comin' deawn,
   An' walkin arm i' arm :
Aw sed they'd blight each other's life,
   If ever they geet wed ;
Neaw nobry would believe o' th' words
   Thad nowty woman sed !

Yet scooars an' scooars may grooap for truth,
   An nod know where to turn ;
An' when aw try to show um t' leet,
   Aw'm coo'd to ill to burn !
Aw know where love an' friendship lies,
   Bi th' shape o' th' head, an th' size :
They'll come no moore o' cheeatin me,
   An' tellin barefaced lies !

Hoo's Two Year Owd To-Morn.

Aw've bin eawr Nelly's slave so long,
    Aw dorn'd want to be free;
Aw'm t' doctor too; when dolly's ill,
    It's awlus browt to me.
An' mony a ugly weawnd aw've stitched
    Wheer t' skin's bin badly torn,
Whol hoo's set like a little queen—
    Hoo's two year old to-morn.

Whene'er hoo's eawt Care snidges reawnd
    Then steyls in like a thief;
When hoo comes back hoo brings in Mirth,
    An' leaves no room for Grief.
Then Hope an' Love con grow an' spread,
    Like scented flowers, 'mong th' corn,
Aw wish hood come; hoo doesn'd know
    Hoo's two year owd to·morn.

It's strikin' eight; hoo'll nod be long
    Afoor hoo shows her face—
So little an' so young, an' yet
    Beawt hor ther's nowt i' th' place.
Beawt hor this life wer bleak and bare—
    Of o' th' choice pleasures shorn;
Hoo's tek her doll an' ride on th' tram—
    Hoo's two year old to morn.

Though t' fire's bin bet aboon an heawr,
   Id hesn'd burnt so breet ;
Till hoo geds up, though th' sun may shine,
   Id corn'd come gradely leet.
Nell, bring thy smiles, an' let's leet up—
   Life's derkest nooks adorn ;
Hoo's here ! Cum, led me tell tha t' fost—
   Tha'rt two year owd to-morn.

Last neet tha'd two times tọ ged up,
   Bud neaw tha's nobbud one ;
Here mammy, reych them clogs of hors,
   Bud led *me* put 'em on.
Ther little neaw, an' eawt at th' tooas,
   An' th' heels is badly worn ;
Tha's hev o pair wi' brass o reawnd—
   Tha'rt two year owd to-morn.

Thy steps aw'll guide whole'er aw live,
   An' even when aw dee ;
Aw feels as aw should turn i' th' grave
   If owt wer hurtin' thee.
Aw'll pick tha t' fleaw'rs fro' t' rooads o' life,
   An' keep tha safe fro' t' thorn ;
My happiest heawrs are spent wi' thee—
   Tha'rt two year old to-morn.

———

May.

Though every month for me's a cherm,
Aw'm fain as Winter's hed his term ;
For thy breath's gradely sweet and werm,—
      Aw like thee, May !
Tha looks best deawn bi 'th owd Stydd ferm
      At break o' day.

Where th' banks o' Ribble's weshed wi' t' flood,
Aw tramped through mony a field and wood ;
Aw see tha's painted every bud
      Wi' dapple green ;
Thad shadin', too, is fairly good,
      Just in between.

An' then, tha browt thi' varnish brush,
An' touched each fleawer, an' bud, an' bush ;
An' music browt for t' lark an' thrush
      To tune their throoats ;
To t' young 'uns, too, when nice an' flush,
      Tha'll gie some nooats.

Tha's smoothed rough spots in mony a place,
An' trimmed um o wi floral lace ;
When aw see th' smile on Nature's face,
      Aw knew tha'd bin ;
Aw feel aw's like o' th' human race
      Sin theaw coom in.

Tha's deckorated Nature's shrine,
Where t' rays o' th' sun neaw dance an shine ;
Tha fairly seems thad dress o' thine,
   So nice an' new ;
Wi daisy spots to intertwine
   Wi' spots o' blue.

———

Musings.

The fluttering of my window blind
 Had wake'd me from a dream ;
I heard my own sweet village bells ;
 I saw a glittering stream ;
There 'neath the bridge I saw it creep ;
Then away it went with a bounding leap.

The blind was white, and decked with fringe,
 And stripes of gauzy fent—
With these the wind had come to play,
 Where shadows came and went !
My home—my native woods, were seen ;
And the Ribble was rolling down between.

Old Time was there so tall and thin,—
 I knew him by his look ;
He show'd one spot he'd left unchanged
 Where Ribble meets the brook ;
There just as when I came away
Were the pebbles strewn on the shining bay.

Yes, there's the shore where Jane and I
   Had wander'd hand in hand ;
And there's the cot of clay I built
   For her upon the sand ;
But soon I saw the gauze unwind,
And the scene was changed on the window blind.

Once more I heard the distant bells
   Could think—could see, and feel—
Could fancy come at such a time,
   And all my senses steal—
If so, I'd leave the world behind,
And for ever gaze on the window blind.

I knew those shadow'd scenes of home,
   And every inch of ground !
Tho' oft the wind would change the scene,
   An' then go whistling round,—
To bring sweet memories for the mind
And to throw them all on the window blind.

Then darkness came, the shadows flit,
   Nor left behind a trace ;
The sun took up a fleecy cloud,
   And threw it o'er his face ;
Then moved to tears he was to find
The shadows were gone from the window blind.

But soon he smiled and dried his tears,
   And threw his veil away ;

D

Then every shadow jumped for joy,
　　And flicker'd in its play ;
The long rod danced to please the wind,
And the shadows flit on the window blind.

Sweet fancy ! When I am alone,
　　Then do thou come to me,—
If e'er I free myself from care,
　　'Tis when I range with thee !
Should friends be false or prove unkind,
I will look with thee on the window blind.

T' Clock as Stan's on Th' Cornish.

Neaw, clock, let's learn fro' tuneful Spring—
　　That's t' singing school for me ;
When t' birds 'll o ther music bring,
　　To chant fro' bush an' tree.
O t' feathered throng 'll swell ther throoats,
　　Fro' t' lark to t' dandy cock ;
Wi' natur's choir aw'll juin mi nooats,
　　If theaw will, larum clock !

But theaw geet cowd at t' broker's shop,
　　Left shiverin' eawt i' th' cowd ;
They wouldn'd tek thee in i' th' pop,
　　They sed theaw wor to owd.

Aw know thi constitution's strong,
    Though neaw theaw looks forlornish ;
I'll shift that cowd afoor so long—
    Theaw'll sweat a bit on th' cornish.

Tho' mony a time fooaks run tha deawn,
    An' med tha stop an' fret ;
If theaw'll throw back to t'·world its freawn,
    Theaw'll win its smiles back yet ;
Sooa whol it's snoorin' fast asleep,
    Nick time for me whol singin' ;
Aw'll do mi nook if theaw'lt just keep
    Thi pendle nicely swingin'.

Aw know thi frame's received a shock,
    But aw'll soon bring tha reawnd ;
Just try thi best at five o'clock,
    To mek thi 'larum seawnd.
I've hed a gradely lookin' up,
    Among mi things i' th' wallet ;
Here tek this oil an' hev a sup,
    I'll try to suit thi *pallet*.

I'm listenin' to thi beatin' heart,
    It's rather faint an' low ;
Bud theigher ! Neaw tha's med a start
    Some signs o' life to show.
Just led mo wesh thi hands an' face,
    An' don this cooat o' varnish ;
Tha'll be an ornament to th' place,
    Tha'll swagger on thad cornish.

An' though theaw wor so bad at th' fost,
    So wake an' stiff i' th' joints ;
Theaw sees tha's welly sin through t' wost,
    For t' time theaw truly points.
Tha's suffered martyrdom sin t' time
    Thi hand wor crushed wi t' rocker.
Bud neaw theaw'rt regular i' thi chime,
    Theaw'rt fairly up to t' *knocker.*

Thi hands an' face is nice an' breet,
    Tha'rt nother slow nor fast ;
I'll wind tha up an' keep tha reet,
    Tha's fun a hooam at last.
An' th' wife hes browt thi things, aw know,
    Hoo's put 'em i' thi case ;
Tha'rt neckin' leawder, just to show,
Tha'rt satisfied wi' th' place.

If theaw wor stopped, aw should feel queer,
    I' th' neet when o's so quate,
Wi' t' cat curled up asleep i' th' cheer,
    An' th' fire burnt deawn i' th' grate ;
It's then aw know thi sharp "tic-tic"
    Is sweetest seawnd con furnish ;
Ther's nowt i' th' place is hofe as wick
    As t' clock as stan's on' th' cornish.

He Sed He Would.

Neaw whether aw succeed or fail,
Aw'm beawn to try to write a tale.
It's true is every word ut's in id,
So neaw aw think aw'd best begin id.
A chap coom reawnd to buy owd lumber,
An' wacken fooak up fro' their slumber.
Owd fooak he's robbed o' mony a nap,
An' childer fown asleep o'er t' pap.
He went abeawt fro' place to place
Wi' reddish nooase an' nasty face.
He seemed to little for his clooase,
He'd nasty rags to cleyn his nooase ;
Bud aw'd bin learn't fro' fooak ut's wise
A chap i' rags to ne'er despise.
Neaw this chap hed a raggy coat,
An' faded muffler reawnd his throoat ;
In fact, he looked a trifle seedy—
A chance for me of helpin' th' needy ;
Aw thowt good luck hed travelled wi' him, .
An' aw wer gradely fain to see him.
To shorten th' tale, an' sooner tell id,
Aw'd lumber, an' wer like to sell id.

Aw wer gradely fagged eawt,
For aw'd hed a rough day,
Aw wer cover'd wi nast,
An aw wanted mi tay,
When this chap give a thump at th' back dooar
He'd a sack on his back,

An' aw thowt in a crack
As he'd buy whod aw hed on to th' flooar.

Bud aw'll nod go for,
Whol aw tell whod id wor.

Aw'd sum owd stockin feet,
As aw'd hed eawt o' th' seet,
An things eawt o' th' cellar an garret,
Ther wer three pair o' shoon,
An an owd broken spoon,
An t' cage as geet broken wi t' parrot.

A swart med o' tin,
An' a dripper put in,
As hed awlus med th' gravy look rusty ;
Sum wheels of a clock,
An' eawr Nelly's owd frock,
As smelled raythcr mildewed an fusty.

Short lengths o' tape,
An' a hat eawt o' shape,
Id wer't th' hat as aw'd hed to be wed in ;
Ther wer pappers an books,
As aw'd fun i' odd nooks,
An' th' pert of eawr Nelly's owd beddin'.

An rags aw reckon'd up bi 'th skoor,
Like little meauntains on to 'th floor ;
Aw roused um up to led um see,
An then aw ses " Whod's price to be ?"
He ses, " I won't be arfther tellin',

But lave it to the man that's sellin."
Aw looked, an' then aw scrat mi head,
An' said " they'd better o' be weighed."
This seemed to give him mental pain,—
He roar'd eawt " Is it way'd yo mane,
Shure I can tell yez to a rag ;"
Wi thad he put um in his bag.
"I'll take these, thin a bag I'll borrow ;
The other lots I'll fetch to-morrow,
Maybe to-day, if 'tisn't rainin,
Then missus can do all her claynin ;
To chate aw'd never yet begin,
For shure t' would be a mortal sin."
Aw knew one bag would never owd um,
An' gradely fain I wor aw'd sowd um.
Aw waits to hear a thump at th' dooar,
For th' things—aw hev um still on th' flooar,
Aw thinks he's comin' every day—
It's three week sin he went away.
Th' wife ses hoo'd sell um if hoo could ;
Aw *know* he'll cum—*he sed he would.*

In Memoriam.

FATHER STEPHEN PERRY, S.J., ASTRONOMER ; Born Aug. 26th, 1833 ; died at Demerara, Jan. 3rd, 1890.

Loud wails of lamentation o'er the land,
    The nations now are plunged in grim dismay ;
For death hath touched him now with icy hand,
    Ere New Year's joyous greetings died away.

Faith brought to him her lamp in early youth,
  To lead through paths of Science's fertile field.
Where'er it grew he culled the flower of truth,
  Then fearless went he forth with virtue's shield.

And patiently he'd watch through darkest night,
  Majestic worlds of wonder oft he'd trace ;
But darkness now for him is changed to light, ·
  And creature meets Creator face to face.

The twinkling stars above no more he'll watch
  Through misty morn and eve to toil and wait,
For angels' fingers now will lift the latch—
  No longer shall he linger at the.gate.

———

Thad heawse into th' Fowd.

Aw'd thrown deawn mi book,
  Aw'd bin moither'd wi' t' din ;
Mi arm cheer i' th' nook
  Aw wer fain to creep in.
Tho' aw like scenes 'uts new,
  Yet mi heart clings to 'th owd,
When mi wants wer so few,
  I' thad heawse into th' fowd.

They'd o' gone to bed,
  Aw wer left bi missel ;
Then fancy soon led
  To a sweet little dell.

Owd Time were rowled back,
   Aw'd no silver nor gowd ;
Aw wer co'd little Jack
   I' thad heawse into th' fowd.

Aw see th' swallows leet
   Where they built under 't thatch ;
Id seawnded so sweet,
   Dud thad click o'th th' owd latch.
Aw crept to 't so quate,
   Whol aw tried to feel bowd ;
Then aw swung back 'th owd gate
   To thad heawse into th' fowd.

My heart id went fast,
   For id o' seemed so plain ;
Aw'd th' present an' th' past
   Wi' o' th' pleasures an' pain.
Ageean aw'm a lad,
   Tho' aw'm fifty year owd ;
Yet aw weave wi' mi dad
   I' thad heawse into th' fowd.

Up owd Strangle Street,
   Just facin' th' brook foot ;
Them watters booath meet,
   As they try to ged to 't.
Aboon th' little teawn,
   When deeath's med me cowd ;
Aw could like to lie deawn
   Near thad heawse into th' fowd.

Eawr Little Nell.

Aw'm fairly upset abeawt thee, Nell !
   Thad cough and thi breathing's so bad ;
Tha morn'd go an' dee like that tother,
   Oh ! dorn'd go an' heart-break thi dad.
Aw feel as aw cudn'd live beawt tha,
   Theaw're sich a fine lass when theaw'rt weel ;
Aw'll nod leave thi side for a minute,
   Except just to write wod aw feel.

Thad tother bud coom on a visit,
   Hoo's gon hooam to th' choir up aboon ;
If they've a wood cheer i' thad mansion,
   Hoo'll sing in't from morning to noon.
Their music's so nice up in Heaven,
   Aw know hoo'll be just in her glee ;
Hoo may happen keep i'th tune, but hoo'll mix id,
   For't part on't ull be abeawt me.

Hoo's towd God o'er me being lonely,
   And moping abeawt on this earth,
So theaw wer sent down as a comfort,
   Tha bundle of mischief and mirth.
When aw look at them things as theaw's played wi,
   Aw feel ther plump teed to my heart ;
Oh ! Nelly, neaw dorn'd go an' leave mo—
   Aw corn'd do wi hevvin' to part.

Cum, just let mo see tha clap blessin's,
  An' point at thad owd 'larum clock,
An' sheawt o' thi dad as theaw use to,
  And let slavver run deawn thi frock.
Theaw would if theaw could, bud theaw'rt sleepy ;
  Theaw'rt better to-day aw con see—
Then cum to thi dad an' he'll rock tha,
  Theaw's bo-peep nice on his knee.

Neaw stop thad machine an' talk quately,
  An' give her a chance o' sum rest ;
Aw know aw look rough, bud aw'm human,
  When childer u'll lean on mi breast.
Aw'm trying mi best to be patient,
  Aw'm tryin' to think hoo'll cum reawnd ;
If hoo dees aw'd rather go wi her,
  An' booath lie together i'th greawnd.

In Blackburn Park

When Spring puts on her gaudy cap,
And fills with flowers fond Flora's lap ;
The fairest spot on Nature's map
        Is Blackburn Park.

Her choice of treasures there she'll bring,—
Her spotted carpet out she'll fling ;
The thrush and blackbird then will sing
        In Blackburn Park.

There, maidens shy their walks will take,
Nor dream of harm, by rock or lake,
Tho' Cupid's darts shall havoc make
      In Blackburn Park.

He sends his darts in lane or street,
Then maidens will their lovers greet,
Yet his own home is Flora's feet
      In Blackburn Park.

If you would life's short day prolong,
Then leave the mad world's giddy throng;
The Robin sings his sweetest song
      In Blackburn Park.

On some old bough, in frost and snow,
He sings his song so sweet and low;
His waistcoat red he's proud to show
      In Blackburn Park.

And tho' sometimes when sorely prest,
He leaves the spot he loves the best,
He comes again to build his nest,
      In Blackburn Park.

'Tis there where children ask to go,
Where flowers in all their beauty grow—
Their daisy bunches oft they'll show
      In Blackburn Park.

'Tis there where towering rocks are seen,
With green spots nestled in between—
A place of beauty, shade, and sheen,
    Is Blackburn Park !

Feb. 23rd, 1889.

— ·· —

Pavin' th' Branch.

Aw've noss'd my papper, pen, an' ink,
An shut my e'en an' tried to think ;
Through th' noise these men hes med eawtside,
Aw've th' headwerch whol aw corn'd abide.
Bud neaw aw think aw'll ged agate,
An' just explain it why aw'm late ;
An' heaw we've o' bin situated
Ay ! patiently for years we've waited.

Aw'd thowt as Blegburn Corporation
Wer't slowest chaps we hed i' th' nation,
Bud though aw thowt as they wer wrong,
Aw'd sense enough to howd mi tongue.
Aw've suffered martyrdom mysell,
An' others if they would but tell ;
When winter coome so cowd an' weet,
Owd fooak it took 'um off their feet ;

When't watter coome i' mony a flood,
An' left us ankle-deep i' mud ;
I' summer time eawr wives geet crusty,
Because o't furniture wer dusty.

Aw could a weary tale unravel
O' fooak uts fown 'mong th' clay an' gravel ;
Whenever th' road geet nice an' hard,
They'd cum an' plough id yard bi' yard.

An' when we'd spells of dryish weather,
They'd never deg for weeks together ;
Bud when derk cleawds begun to show,
They'd bring thad thing an' deg id o'.
Bud men, an' angels too, hev stumbled,
We've bin like Job, an' never grumbled ;
An' neaw wer geddin' whod we've craved,
For th' Mayor ses neaw it's to be paved.

O' big square stooans ther's mony a skoor,
Ther, o' piled up at front o' th' door,
Beside big hoyles as looks like caves,
Or like sum gred long narrow graves.
O't childer when they cum fro' t' skoo,
They try ther best whod they con do ;
Aw've sin um giving mony a lift—
When th' men cums back they hev to shift.

But th' street, fooak co's id Branch Rooad yet,
Where trees deawn th' sides once waved an' met ;
Ther's heawses neaw an' shops, an' pubs,
Where once grew flowers and bushy shrubs,
Where lovers then would wend ther way
I'th' benny months o' June or May,
An' then seet under th' trees to rest,
Whol th' skylark carolled o'er his nest ;

Where't bees on mony a flower would leet
Wi drowsy hum tor't th' edge o' neet :

Where 't lambs once gambled, gay an' free,
An't t' fruit once hung fro' bush an' tree ;
An' dewdrops shining on to th' flowers,
An' th' rooasebuds hung i' woodland bowers,
Where th' stockdove flutterin' to its nest,
Whol th' sun wer' paintin' scenes i' th' west ;
Then foxgloves could be fun i' th' glade ;
Bud O, that scrapin' noise fro' t' spade,
I' th' stead o' th' cuckoo's farewell nooat—
" Here, dash id, mopus, reach thad cooat !"

An' mony a time aw've left mi book.
To gooa eawtside an' hev a look,
For t' noises gooa on o' through th' day,
Next week aw think they'll be away.
An' when it's dun aw'll swagger deawn,
Aw's know it's nicest street i' th' teawn ;
Tom, pick them papers off thad floor,
Oh ! drat thad noise—aw'll write no moore.

June, 1890

A Flittin'.

A rollin' stooan, it's awlos sed,
  Con never gether moss,
But them as rowls is awlus clean—
  Aw corn'd see heaw ther woss,

An' aw've just moved fro' t' derk to t' leet,
　　An' though aw've nod mich wit,
Aw think aw've sence enough to know,
　　It's nicer wheer aw've flit.

An' heaw we geet o' th' things across,
　　Aw's hev a job to tell,
Aw'd men aw paid to carry sum,
　　An' sum aw took misell.
As where aw've gon's nod fifty yerds,
　　Aw dud beawt kert or tit,
For th' naybours gi' mo mony a lift,
　　Wi' helpin' mo to flit.

My wife, aw couldn'd ged her eawt,
　　Hoo'd sitch a nasty face ;
Mi goods o' seem'd to walk abeawt
　　To try to find a place ;
An'th rockin' cheers, booath wife's an' mine,
　　Ther'll noather on um fit ;
They look as if they'd booath foo'n eawt
　　Because they've hed to flit.

My cheor stan's i'th place o'th wife's,
　　An hor's where mine should be ;
A'stid o' me bein facin th' wife,
　　My wife sits facin' me.
Eawr Nelly's cried booath neet an' day,
　　Hoo'll nother lie nor sit,
Yo see hoo's nobbut youngish yet,
　　Hoo hes'nd sence to flit.

An' whod aw hev to tell yo' neaw
  Aw know yo'll think it's chaff,
For when mi teeam wer o' at work,
  They med four paysons laugh ;
When th' dolly tub cum walkin' deawn
  Aw thowt they'd hev a fit ;
Eawr Tom hed sence to sneeze inside,
  To led um know we'd flit.

When th' childer cooam aw leet um stert
  To carry whod wer leet,
An' twenty-five went late for 't shoo,
  An' others stopped whol neet ;
Ther arms wer twinin' reawnd mi legs—
  " Hey, mon I help a bit ?"
Aw could'nd help bud led um stert
  O' helpin' mo to flit.

An' one o' th' chaps as paves i' th' Branch,
  As werks reet facin' th' dooar,
He hung his meyt up on a nail—
  He'd left id there afore ;
Bud this time sumbry took id o,
  Beside his hat an' kit,
Aw think id's sumbody eawt o' werk,
  As wants to larn to flit.

June, 1890.

E

𝔄 Sweet 𝔏ittle Spot.

Such a sweet little spot,
It can ne'er be forgot ;
Round my heart are its mem'ries entwined,
Where the brook wanders by,
With the Ribble so nigh,
And the people so homely and kind.
It was there, when a boy,
That my heart leapt with joy,
When aw'd finished my cut or my beam ;
Then away from my home,
By their waters to roam,
For the sand martin's nest by the stream.

Then I've come back again,
Up that shady old lane,
Where I knew every inch of the track ;
To that sunny Greenside,
I have tramped it with pride,
With my nettles slung over my back.
They were all my world's wealth,
But I'd freedom and health ;
I could soar above sorrow supreme ;
In that long narrow room
I could sing at my loom
In that old-fashioned cot by the stream.

By that old bobbin mill,
Where the water 's so still,
I have gone with my pinhook and rod ;

I was filled with delight
When the fishes would bite
At the worm I'd found under the sod.
But there's mills large and new
Where wild roses once grew,
And the looms are all driven by steam ;
Now, the Ribble will roar,
But 'twill sparkle no more
As it did when I waded the stream.

Ah ! But where is that well,
Where the apples once fell—
Those red ones so juicy and sweet ?
Then I loved a strong wind,
For to me it was kind,
When the apples it brought to my feet.
But the well is now dry,
And I heave a deep sigh,
As I think of my boyhood's sweet dream ;
When I watched its o'erflow
To the brook it would go,
For they both loved the Ribble's bright stream.

An Epistle.

Aw write this dark November day
To ax tha why tha stops away ;
Hes ta nod a cheerful word to say,
Does't know as aw've a tumor ?

It's two months neaw sin id begun,
We nod one cheerin' ray fro't sun;
It hurts mo, mon, to see fooak shun
    Mo neaw, 'cause aw've a tumor.

Aw dud ged eawt a bit at fost,
Bud neaw, aw think, it's come to t' wost,
For day an neet id will be noss't,
    Aw'm like to suit mi tumor.

Inside or eawt ther's nowt bud gloom,
Reminding one o' deeath an t' toome,
An here aw'm limpin' reawnd mi room,
    To try to quaten th' tumor.

Aw've hed slow fayver, t' geawt, an't tic,
Rheumatic pains—bin drunken sick,
Bud never nowt sin aw wer wick,
    To match these pains o' t' tumor.

Last neet when comin' hooam aw fell,
Aw've hed them there, tha's heeard mi tell ;
O'th plagues ther is eawtside o' hell,
    Ther'e nooan to match a tumor.

Aw've doctors tried i' mony a teawn,
Yet still aw'm limpin' up an deawn;
If aw wer a king aw'd part wi't creawn,
    If aw could part wi' t' tumor.

Aw's nod give up nor pine an fret,
For troubles fly when bravely met,
An life hes charms to offer yet,
    If aw could rid this tumor.

Theaw dud'nd fret o'er t' shuttle peg,
'Theaw sung of t' peeark wi' t' brokken leg ;
Tho' this o' mine wer bud a seg,
    Its rippen'd to a tumor.

An tho' aw'm nod a bird o' nooat,
When spring time comes aw'll cast mi cooat,
Then safe thro't meawt aw'll chirp a nooat,
    To bid farewell to t' tumor.

An neaw, owd friend, tha knows mi case ;
Dorn'd keawr so long i' th' " Thrysting Place,"
Bud come i' th' Branch an show thi face—
    Oh ! another twitch o' th' tumor.

                  Dec. 1st, 1888.

Hoo's Set Off a Walkin' To-day.

Aw've bin watchin' eawr Nelly o day,
   As hoo's toddled abeawt on her feet ;
An aw've nooaticed each dimple go less,
   Whol her face grew quite solemn tor't neet.
But hoo'd fown fast asleep i' mi arms,
   As Owd Sol had just thrown his last ray ;
An' I hope sleep'll give her new strength,
   For hoo's set off a-walkin' to-day !

Ay, hoo's getten sitch pearly white teeth,
  But hoo doesn'd eat butties so fast,
For hoo weets um an waves um i'th air,
  An hoo rubs um i' o sooarts o' nast.
An' hoo's life's roughest broo yet to climb,
  Wi' sitch tornin's to leead her astray ;
Oh, mi heart'll fair werch when aw think
  As hoo's set off a-walkin' to-day !

But to hor life is th' breetest side up,
  It's on me its dark shadows is cast ;
An' to-neet aw do wish aw could think
  As her smiles would stick to her to t' last.
Among 't number ut hoo'll meet upo' th' rooad,
  There'll be wastrels as study foul play ;
There's sitch dangers i' th' corners o' life,
  An hoo's set off a-walkin' to-day !

Neaw they've ta'en her away for o t' neet,
  An' they've left mo deawn here bi misel ;
Aw feel ill when hoo's eawt o' mi seet,
  For hoo's part o' mi life is eawr Nell.
Whol ther's th' angels on guard reawnd her bed,
  Aw'll go up an' aw'll ask um to stay,
An to guide every step as hoo teks,
  For hoo's set off a-walking to-day !

Led her catch mornin's sunshine o' life,
  For on me it's a long way past noon ;
Bud aw'll keep a firm grip of her hond,
  If grim fate doesn'd part us too soon.

Tho' aw corn'd hope to see her to th' end,
   Aw con tek her agate on her way ;
An aw'll give her o th' leet aw con ged,
   For hoo's set off a-walking to-day !

Soa aw'll try hard to shake off this gloom,
   An aw'll keep up mi head i' life's race ;
For aw think we con banish Despair,
   An' he'll fly when he see's her breet face.
O her smiles aw'll lock up i' mi heart,
   For they'll keep id fro' grief an decay ;
Bud aw'll pay um o back as we go,
   For hoo's set off a-walking to-day !

Feb. 13th, 1890.

Faces in the Fire.

The outside world is hushed and still,
   The loved one's all in bed ;
My chair I've drawn up close beside
   The fire so bright and red.
Let fancy with love's fingers try
   To strike the tuneful lyre ;
     And perhaps a note
     There may be taught
By faces in the fire.

Oh, bring to-night each missing link
   I've lost from memory's chain ;
Let forms and faces long forgot
   Now visit me again.

With magic hand they lift the latch—
   Some come while some retire ;
      Each face I know
      That in its glow
   Looks radiant in the fire.

That thin and careworn face, I know,
   Had earn'd a perfect rest ;
My troubles soothed in early life,
   And lulled me on her breast.
My brother's come to me again,
   My dull brain to inspire ;
      For one short while
      I see him smile
   With faces in the fire.

That old boathouse I know it well,
   So red's the ouside wall ;
And there's the village schoolhouse, too,
   Among the poplars tall.
But oh ! that blaze has spoiled them all,
   There goes the church and spire ;
      Thus while I sit
      My pleasures flit
   With faces in the fire.

And like the fire my life has been ;
   In youth 'twas all aglow ;
As age creeps on the vital spark
   Is burning dim and low.

But mirth shall try to fan the flame
    Until it doth expire,
       Like that last spark
       When all is dark,
    Like faces in the fire.

Dick !

Aw connod sing o'er heroes bowd,
    Ut feyt i' forren parts,
For't thowts o'th widows left at hooam,
    To dee o' brokken hearts,
Whol nation's hev bin bowt an' sowd,
To furnish few wi' fame an' gowd ! .

Ther's mony a cleawn as th' world' drest up,
    Wi' medals on his breast ;
An' mony a poor neglected grave,
    Wheer heroes lie at rest :
Aw'll sing o'er one ut's weel an' wick—
Despised, neglected, silly Dick !

Neaw Dick's as simple as a child ;
    He's awlus bin content,
Tho' poverty hes follow'd him,
    Whichever way he went :
At skoo he could'nd pay his fee,
An never learnt his A B C.

Ther's grown up looak ut's rather daft,
   Like—hes'nd wit to jooak ;
They sheawt " Oh, Peg," whol childer's learnt,
   To mimic th' owder fooak,—
They dorn'd gie Dick his gradely name,
Because they hev'nd sense to shame.

O' th' by-way pads is known to Dick,
   For miles an' miles areawnd ;
He knows each ferm an' public heawse,
   An' every inch o' th' greawnd ;
At walking too, he's bad to lick,
Ther's few con keep at t' front o' Dick.

When we lived deawn at th' owd Greenside,
   When he, like us, wer pooar ;
Aw knew when he'd a soft ooatcake,
   Bi' th' way he oppen'd th' dooar !
He'd cum an say, as if wi' fear,
" Tha corn'd guess whod aw've getten here !"

Aw'd guess, an though aw knew o t' time,
   Aw'd keep on guessin' fast,
Till nearly everything aw'd named—
   " Ooatcake " I'd say at last !
An then a laugh, an sheawt o glee,
An th' cake wer landed on mi knee !

An' th' world wer praising me because
    Aw'd sense to watch an' wait ;
Whol he wer doin' good bi stealth,
    Aw practised foul desate ;
An tho' th' world's gin him th' freawn an'th kick,
It's praised woss fooak than silly Dick.

An' though he's reckon'd short o' brains,
    An' never learnt to read,
Ther's one good lesson as he's learnt,
    That's helpin' fooak i' need :
Whol ther's a child near him ut's sick,
Ther's nod mitch sleep for silly Dick.

When knowledge seet her table eawt,
    An put o' th' dainties on,
An stood theer waitin' wi' a smile,
    To welcome everyone—
When wealth cum in, an' hed his pick,
There worn'd mitch left for silly Dick !

Aw've heeard o'er One as coome deawn here,
    To ged fooak free fro' sin ;
Like little childer they'd to be,
    An then he'd tek um in,—
He knows o' th' fooak booath deead an' wick—
Aw think He'll find a place for Dick !

God bless tha, Dick, an' help tha throo,
    An' when tha cums to dee,
'Tha's nod as mitch to answer for,
    As stuck-up fooak like me !
An' when life's Ribble's booated o'er,
Ther's nicer sands on t' to'ther shore !

Owd Shakespeare ses as th' world's a stage,
    An' life is bud a play,—
Another mon he ses its bud
    A journey of a day ;
When he's put deawn his spoon an stick,
Aw know ther'll be a place for Dick !

June, 1891.

In Memoriam.

EDWIN WAUGH.

Born January 29th, 1817, died April 30th, 1890.

The words '· He's-dead" refuse to leave the tongue ;
    Wayfarers here are left in deepest gloom.
A star hath fallen from the world of song,
    Grim death has been and claimed him for the tomb.

But ere he went he left a rich bequest,
    And those who loved h'm most desire no more ;
The bird hath piped all day, then found his nest,
    The barque has landed safe upon the shore.

Then bear him forth with measured step and slow,
   The sable crowd in tears will open wide ;
Oh ! make his grave where meadow flowers may grow,
   Now all his earthly load he's laid aside.

Yes, crape the harp and strike the muffled drum,
   No more for him the heather branches wave ; ·
With softest music let the mourners come,
   And bring their wreaths to deck a poet's grave.

———

A Cat's Tale.

Attend to mi' *mews*, an aw'll rhyme yo' mi' wail,
Aw'll *tickle* yo'r fancy wi' t' end o' mi' tale ;
Neaw cats hes their fortunes o' gin eawt bi' fate,
Which leeads mo to think as mi' mother went late ;
      This part's verra sad,
      Aw ne'er knew mi' dad—
Aw think he'll hev cleyn'd his last plate.

Aw'll nod tell o'er t' gossips as use to come in,
Nor't scandal they swallow'd, wi' t' ale, rum, or gin ;
An' th' mischief they med, aw should think yo con guess,
Ther tales they went longer, as th' rum id went less.
      Whod lies they would tell !
      They damaged thersell
Bi' barrin' th' highway to success.

Aw liked th' place at fost—among th' wosted aw'd play,
Whey they butter'd m' feet just to ged mo to stay ;
Bud neaw aw'm neglected, th' milks o' in a clot,
Mi' heart id fair heaves when aw see id i'th pot.
        Eh ! when aw'd new milk,
        Mi cooat wer like silk ;
Hoo'd six—aw wer't nicest i' th' lot.

Aw hev med mistakes, an lost mony a stiff race,
An then aw've hed th' wiskers o' rubbed off my face ;
It's hard when one's ill to be leather'd reawnd th' hoyle,
To be med in a mop an then thrown among th' coyle ;
        Aw know as it's wrong,
        Aw'll nod stan id long,
Mi' beauty ther trying to spoil.

Aw'm happy sometimes, an' con join i' ther mirth,
Of a neet when ther telling ther tales up o'th hearth ;
When th' fire's shining breet, aw con bask in its ray,
An o' seems at rest after t' troubles o' th' day ;
        On th' rug aw con sit,
        As't dark shadows flit,
Like time as keeps passin' away.

To Autumn.

Eh ! me, booath Spring an' Summer's gone,
An' th' fleawers keep fadin' one by one,
Aw'll homple eawt whol'er aw con,—
        Id does mo good
To see thad dress as tha's put on
        I' th' field an' wood.

Tha's shown as t' seeds worn'd sown i' vain
Bi th' fruit tha's browt an' th' gowden grain,
An' weshed so clear wi' dew an' rain,
     An' Summer's tears ;
Whol th' robin sung i' plair-tive strain
     O' changin' years.

Aw think when Sol his gowd beams threw,
Them shades o' thine tha's mixed wi' t' dew,
There's summat quare if one bud knew,
     Tha's stown 'em o,—
Bud heaw tha dyed 'em as they grew
     Aw's never know.

Aw've stored thy fruits i' th' nicest room,
An' buried Spring an Summer's bloom.
Thy leeaves is nice to spread o'er th' tomb
     Wher th' wind con play,
An' music mek whol Winter's gloom
     Hes past away.

Like flowers we hev eawr June an' May ;
When Autumn comes we're tinged wi' gray,—
We bud an' bloom, then fade away.
     Life's storms will rave,
An' we're bud med o' bits o' clay,
     To throw i' th' grave.

1890.

November.

Aw'm cheer'd wi' t' blue i' th' sky aboon,
   Thro' every month i' th' year ;
Whol tha' comes in an' throws thad vail
   O' darkness everywhere :
Tho' January may be dark,
   An' winter-born December,
Ther is no month as black as thee,
   For shame, for shame, November.

Aw hed a Robin used to come,
   Thro' mony a winter's snow ;
Bud neaw he's deead, no more he'll sing,
   For me on th' backyard wo,—
Aw'd live o' fish, an' fast, an' pray,
   If every day wer Ember,
An' be content if rid o' thee,
   Theaw mournful, meawled November !

Aw'm fond o th' leet ; aw corn'd like thee,—
   Tha's darkened Nature's face ;
Sooa go thi ways, December, then,
   May come an' tek thi place.
Wi' shadows glidin' o' thro' th' place,
   It's like a haunted chamber ;
Tha'd vex a saint wi' thy black looks,
   Tha' growlin' grim, November !

An' poets—them as fratch o'er thee,
　They corn'd bi gradely reet ;
Tha hes no mind to co thi own—
　Tha'rt changin', day an' neet !
Aw've reckon'd up fro' being a lad,
　O' th' pleasures aw remember ;
Nod one thro' thee, hes come to me,
　Tha nasty, dark, November !

An' look heaw th' leeaves hes curled and dee'd,
　An' dropp'd fro' bush an' tree :
Led Time bud tek another stride,
　An' then we're shut o' thee !
Them varied shades as look'd so weel,
　Thro' August an' September—
They're spoil'd an' trampled under t' feet,
　An' o thro' thee, November !

Ther's nobbut four i' o eawr lot,
　To reckon young an' owd ;
Sin tha coome in we'n every one,
　Bin smoother'd in a cowd :
Tha's brought thi nasty fogs an' rain,
　An' upset every member ;
Aw think owd Blegburn's derk enough,
　Ged eawt, tha black November !

1890.

F

Young Ninety-One.

" Jack, poo thi cheer a bit tort mine,
    Let's booath stop up o neet ;
Aw'll thrutch th' owd cerpet under t' door
    To keep th' draught off thi feet."
We seet an' camped, led mony a skeeom ;
    Aw fell asleep an' hed a dreeam.

Aw thowt aw heard a gentle knock ;
    Aw went an' oppen'd th' dooar,
When Ninety-One coome glidin' in,
    An' dropped his pack on t' floor.
Just then Hope whisper'd i' mi ear,
" A welcome give—that's eawr New Year."

" Aw will," aw ses, quite fain as Hope
    Were theer to keep me reet ;
Aw press'd his hand, an' pointed deawn
    To th' bundle at his feet.
An' sed, "Neaw, would you be so kind
    As t' oppen thad an' ease mi mind ? "

His face an' form aw corn'd describe ;
    He wore a sword an' creawn ;
He wouldn'd tell mo whod he'd brought
    For me an' th' fooak i' th' teawn.
An' when he see mo steyl a look,
He waved mo back to th' cheer i' th' nook.

Aw dud then whod aw'd never dun
    Before i' o' mi life ;
Aw med a speech abeawt Owd Time,
    An' introduced mi wife.

Th' wife blush'd an' stagger'd tort his pack ;
He raised his hand an' waved her back.

At last aw thowt, aw'd ax him plain ;
   He'd answer Yes or No :
Aw sed, "Whod hes to in thad pack
   Neaw will to led us know?
We'r living neaw i' fear and deawt,
   Untee them knots an' oppen eawt."

He smiled, an' then he shaked his heyd,
   An' walked away wi' th' pack ;
Aw jumped on to mi feet at once
   To try to fotch him back.
Th' wife coome an' push'd mo back i' th' cheer,
An' ses, " Tha'rt dreaming o'er t' New Year."

Aw scrat my head an' rubbed mi een,
   An' then aw tried to think ;
Aw went to bed, geet up ageean,
   An' couldn'd sleep a wink.
My wife then towd mo o aw'd sed—
Aw wrooate id eawt an' went to bed.

Owd fooak like me is best i' bed,
   Let th' young 'uns watch an' wait ;
Aw shouldn'd like to try ageean
   To reckon up mi fate;
An' as Owd Time keeps peylin' on,
   Aw'll trust to thee, young Ninety-One.

The Moorland Stream.

I saw it in my ramble,
　And poesy bade me stay
To see it sport and gamble,
　So merry in its play.
The robin sang above it,
　And seemed to feel the charm ;
The wagtail said, " I love it,"·
　As it wanders by the farm.

In youth I played with Ribble,
　And knew each mossy nook.
Where it would pause and dribble,
　Just where it met the brook ;
Far from its home the fountain
　Where Nature's beauties swarm ;
I've traced it from the mountain
　'Till it wandered by the farm.

Its moorland home was shaded
　With purple heather bloom ;
But when the foxglove faded,
　'Twas chosen for their tomb.
Rude winter would dissemble,
　It fled in great alarm ;
It seemed to fret and tremble,
　As it wandered by the farm.

What wild sweet tangled places
　It creeps through on its way ;
Kind Nature holds the traces,
　And lets it frisk and play.

It knows not danger's troubles ;
   'Tis nursed on Nature's arm,
Where it will laugh in bubbles
   As it wanders by the farm.

'Twill teach me rhyme and measure,
   When songbirds chant their lay ;
Where Spring unfolds her treasure
   For bright-and beauteous May.
The flowers have all been sleeping,
   While Winter's had his term :
But now they're shyly peeping,
   As it wanders by the farm.

A bright and dashing rover,
   Which often came that way,
" Our single life is over,"
   In rippling rhyme did say ;
" I've wandered far to greet thee,
   Will't keep thy true love warm ?
And every day I'll meet thee,
   And we'll wander by the farm."

                     March 30th, 1889.

An Epistle from Douglas.

Neaw, th' fost thing aw'll explain mi case—
Aw'm ill; aw've hed to change mi place ;
For weeks an' weeks aw've hed a cowd,
But th' doctor ses aw'm geddin' owd ;

He felt mi pulse an' tried mi breath,
An' med mo gradely feared o' death.
He give mo physic an' a pill,
An' if I mend aw's pay his bill ;
Aw hev sum stuff to guggle th' throttle,
He put thad in another bottle.
Aw use id, then it's thrown away,
But th' physic ta'en three times a day ;
He towd mo aw'd to give up study,
An' ged away where t' land wer woody ;
Sooa th' good aw'll sooart fro' whod he sed,
An' th' t'other part aw's soon forged.
When th' wife aw towd, aw see id shocked her,
Hoo ses "Tha'rt like to go bi th' doctor,"
Th' owd lass hoo seem'd fair brocken-hearted,
Aw kussed her twice an' then aw sterted.

Sooa in t' big ship aw sailed away,
An' here aw am i' Douglas bay ;
Aw've hed a verra pleasant sail,
Wi' mony a jooak an' merry tale,
An' comic songs wi' roars o' laughter ;
Aw felt quite lively th' mornin' after.
Aw'm weel enough to write a letter,
Aw's try a poem when aw'm better.
If aw could buy thad jewel health,
Aw'd pay for 't wi' mi worldly wealth ;
Neaw print this letter if it's needed,
There's happen odd uns as u'll read it.

Aw would'nd write abeawt mi'sell,
If aw'd sum gradely news to tell ;

Ther's one thing though aw morn'd forged,
We've two young fooak new getten wed.
Ther nice but rather peevish fooak,
For whod they've dun's aboon a jooak.
Aw'll grumble cause aw've sum occasion,
Aw've just o'er heeard o' th' conversation ;
They've towd th' fooak here aw rhymes a bit,
Bud th' misses hes'nd med mo flit.
" Well ! Well ! " hoo ses, " aw'm nod that sooar,
Aw've hed him lodgin' here afoor,
Aw know th' chap is'nd gradely mad,
Beside he's never hed id bad ;
We'll just try if we corn'd arrange,
He's harmless, though aw know he's strange ;
He seems to stare a deal at nowt,
Aw think thad shows a want o' thowt ;
He's rather strange like in his way,
An' lives beawt sugar in his tay."

Bud neaw aw'm geddin' use to th' shop,
An' if th' price suits aw think aw's stop ;
Beside aw feel aw'm mendin' fust—
Aw'll stop as long as th' brass u'll last.

When aw wer young, eh thad wer't time,
Aw gloried then these hills to climb,
Bud neaw aw know aw'm geddin' owd
Aw dorn'd feel quite as brisk and bowd.
Aw'm waker neaw, nod quite as silly,
Aw'd rather hev id nod so hilly ;
If aw'd my way aw'd hev id flat,
An' screw a tail to every cat.

Ther foreign fooak is th' natives here,
They tawk to fast, an' rather queer ;
O'th Fridays here's unlucky days,
Ther supersticious i' ther ways,
They've bigger moons to shine at neet ;
Ther weather is'nd quite as weet.
O' them wi' ships they co'n um skippers,
A deeal o'th fooak here lives o' kippers ;
But th' mackeral here is fresh an' fatter,
An' their sun rises eawt o'th' watter.
Aw live near th' tower as stans i' th' bay,
Where th' ocean waves oft cunr to play ;
I'th neet-time when aw'm led i' bed
Aw hear um dash on Douglas Head.
An' when aw've dropped i' th' arms o' sleep,
Aw feel's aw'm rocked abeawt on th' deep.
I' th' neet id cries wi' mournful voices,
An' then when mornin' comes rejoices.
At neet id tells mo fooak it's dreawned,
I' th' mornin' teks fooak hooamward beawnd.

An' neaw mi letter to conclude,
At comin' here aw've never rued ;
An' sooa aw'll say no mooar at present ;
Fro' owd Jack Rowkley, Marlo' Crescent.

                                    July, 1890.

_____

There's Hooan Like Yon o' Mine.

There's nowt i' th' world aw like so weel
    As childer nice an' young ;
No seawnd to me is hofe so sweet
    As th' music fro ther tongue.

An' when they climb up on mi knee,
   Ther little arms entwine,
      Aw like um o,
      But still aw know
   Ther's nooan like yon o' mine.

This world wer like a barren plain,
   Where nowt could grow or thrive;
Where fooak would grooap abeawt for th' grave,
   An' hardly feel alive;
Bud when these childer's planted eawt,
   As stars o' love they shine.
      Though mony a skooar
      Will pass bi th' door,
   There's nooan as nice as mine.

To watch 'em meet ther dads an' mams
   When comin' hooam at neet;
There's now't i' books con soften th' heart
   Like watchin' when they meet.
An' as aw write, yon's little Jane,
   Wi' oather eight or nine;
      Ther' full o' fun,
      As breet as th' sun,
   Bud nod as breet as mine.

Ther's one u't lives aboon eawr heawse,
   Hoo passes every day;
An' when hoo stops away fro' t' skoo
   Wi' me hoo'll romp an' play.

A game at hob-scotch suits her t' best,
    When mine just stops on't line.
        Her dance o' glee,
        Aw like to see—
    Hoo s nod as brisk as mine.

Eawr Nelly hings her head so shy,
    Her smile ther's nooan so sweet ;
Hoo's breet as ony summer's sky,
    Or rooase-bud dript wi' weet.
An' them fooak corn'd be gradely reet,
    As says they've one as fine ;
        They morn'd tell me,
        For corn'd aw see
    Ther's nooan like yon o' mine.

𝔍n 𝔐emoriam.

E L I Z A   C O O K.

Born 1818 ; Died September 24th, 1889.

She is not dead—though millions are in grief.
    With all the flowers she sang of deck her grave !
The reaper of the muse has bound her sheaf,
    Let " Buttercups and Daisies " o'er her wave.

Thou art not dead—we have thy muse's flame,
    That heart is still—thou'st left the world's rude throng
On earth for ever—" Hallowed be thy name,"
    'Twill brighter be as Time shall roll along.

The "Old Arm Chair" is vacant now I ween ;
  The harp, its strings are broke, its music fled.
Tread softly o'er each place where she has been ;
  Her spirit lingers there—she is not dead.

From early youth I've loved her tuneful lay ;
  Now cross her hands upon her peaceful breast ;
The sun has set, now fades the lingering day,
  So lay her gently down and let her rest.

Farewell to May.

We shall awlus mek thee welcome,
  Tha's sich nice an sunny sheawers ;
An' tha never misses comin'
  Wi thi brat brimful o' fleawers ;
Whey tha brings um o' for presents,
  An' tha leeaves um on th' way ;
Aw's try to think tha'rt we us,
  Tho' aw know tha's gon' away.

When' th' cuckoo towd us deawn i' th' wood,
  He'd come to welcome thee,
O'th leeaves begun to clap their hands,
  An' fairly danced wi glee ;
A concert sterted then 'mong'th birds,
  An' fooak hed now't to pay ;
They corn'd sing quite as merry neaw,
  They know tha's gon' away.

If life wer med o' winters cowd,
   Then aw should soon retire ;
Bud mony a glimpse does fancy show
   O' thee i' th' winter's fire ;
Aw thinks it's thy breet sunshine, an'
   Aw sings a merry lay ;
When'th cinders drop eawt one by one,
   Aw know tha's gon' away.

Aw'm sorry as tha's hed to leeave,
   Them flowers o' thine u'll fade ;
Primrooases as aw like so weel,
   Are witherin' deawn i'th glade.
Ther's some i'th heart tha's planted,
   Hev blossom'd where they'll stay ;
I' memory fast, whol life shall last,
   They shall never go away.

Them bluebells, heaw they hing ther heads,
   Them colour'd spots i'th wood ; ,
Aw thowt aw see um shiver, when
   Aw tried to find a bud ;
O'th gress looks bent an' seedy neaw,
   An'th lambs forged to play ;
They corn'd be quite as lively, for
   They know tha's gone away.

June, 1890.

Cum Next Sunday Morning.

When owd Sol's climed up eawt o'th' east
　An' o'er hill tops he's peeping,
Aw'll claim mi share o' Nature's feast
　As th' mist o'er th' land is creepin.
Aw know aw hev a friend or two
　As reads mi rhymin' scribble ;
If t' reet uns come, an' just enoo',
　We'll ramble deawn to th' Ribble.

Its getten to far on i'th' week
　To write by card or letter ;
Id nobbut needs a bit o' cheek
　To try a way uts better.
Ther's mony a place aw'm preawd to show
　Where't Ribble's awlus wander'd ;
Aw've fun a way to let you know,
　Aw'll write to th' *Blegburn Standard.*

If Spring's new suit yo' want to see,
　It's free to every comer,
Where Nature decks each bush an' tree
　So nice i' Spring an' Summer.
But let's gooa neaw whol busy May
　Is Ribble's banks adorning ;
Aw've bin afoor, aw'll show yo' t' way,
　Sooa cum next Sunday morning.

Deawn by-way paths bi th' Ribble's side,
    Owd wo's an' hedges climbin',
O'er rindlin' streams to jump or stride—
    Aw'm fain aw geet thad rhyme in.
An' if aw should ged wrong i'th' track,
    It's place as aw wer born in ;
Aw'll wriggle reet beawt turnin' back,
    Sooa cum next Sunday morning.

Where t' song birds gooa to build ther nest,
    Ther screened fro't cowdest weather ;
Owd Ribble valley suits um t' best,
    An' neaw ther just i' feather.
Sooa cum away fro t' smooky teawn
    Where men each other's scornin' ;
Where th' air's so clear, thad's where aw'm beawn,
    Sooa cum next Sunday morning.

Th' owd willow's donn'd his greenest coat,
    Where t' blackbird will be singin' ;
We'll try to just ged deawn to't boat
    As th' owd church bells is ringin'.
Deawn theer ther's sum o' th' richest land,
    Wi barley, wheeat, an' corn in ;
To see 't fro't booat it's fairly grand,
    Sooa cum next Sunday mornin'.

May, 1890.

A Greeting.

Old Year ! thou'lt soon be gone for ever;
　　Time hath made thee travel fast ;
So get thee gone, Fate will not sever
　　All sweet memories of the past.
When at thy birth I danced with gladness,
　　Hope had shown her brightest ray,
Though now my looks have more of sadness,
　　For it is mirth I'd court to-day.
So I'll laugh and I'll sing,
May the New Year bring
New pleasures to dry every tear.
All your readers I greet,
Though we never may meet,
I wish them a Happy New Year.

　　　　　　　　　December 28th, 1889.

————

Let's Booath Poo One Way.

Aw think ther's summat ails tha, Jack,
　　Just look mo straight i'th' face ;
On thee aw've never turned mi back,
　　Bud kept abreast i'th' race.
It's thirty year sin we wer wed—
　　Id will be come next May ;
Neaw dorn'd forged them words tha sed,
　　An' let's booath poo one way.

When theaw took me to th' church, mi lad,
    Thad hard fast knot to tee ;
Tha took mo' then for t' good an't bad,
    An' aw dud same wi thee.
Tho' neaw thi step's nod quite so firm,
    An' aw'm nod quite as gay,
Eawr hearts are quite as true an' warm,
    Sooa let's booath poo one way.

To-neet aw'll speyk just whod aw feel,
    Aw want thee to do't same ;
For if th' world doesn'd use tha weel,
    Tha knows aw'm nod to blame.
Before aw'd see tha want for owt,
    Aw'd werk booath neet an' day ;
Sooa Jack just do neaw tek a thowt,
    An' let's booath poo one way.

Theaw morn'd feight single-handed, mon,
    I'th' world ther's nowt bud strife ;
Let th' best o' friends do whod they con,
    They corn'd do like a wife.
I'th' bits o' jars I know aw'm th' start,
    Whol th' passion's gone away ;
An' then a'm wishing fro' mi heart
    We booath hed poo'd one way.

Theaw'rt bud a stranger, Jack, i'th' world,
    They see tha neaw an' then ;
To me thi life is o' unfurled,
    Theaw'rt nooan o'th' wost o' men ;

So try an' cheer up fro' to-neet,
    Theaw'lt see we's wark eawr way ;
We'll mek th' rough wheels o' life run sweet,
    We'll awlus poo one way.

Sooa cheer up neaw, aw know tha con,
    For tho' theaw'rt rayther blunt ;
Theaw's won life's battles one by one,
    An' awlus kept to t' frunt.
Just tek thi walks deawn Ribbleside,
    An' hear't thrush sing its lay ;
Then tek thi place as t' prop an' guide,
    An' let's booath poo one way.

Gloomy June.

Aw wonder will id ever give o'er rainin',
    Id doesn'd look as ever id would stop ;
Where'e'r aw go to, fooak are o' complainin',
    An' th' hay, it's beawn to spoil id every crop.

Aw should be seechin' sum cool spot to lurk on,
    I'stead o' thad aw've burnt mi breeches knees ;
It's as cowd as th' stooan bottle wi' a cork on,
    If id geds ony cowder id ull freeze.

Id seems to me ther's nowt i'th world bud trouble,
    There's nowt bud gloom—aw've looked fro' east to west ;
In't field o' life there's nowt bud stooan an' stubble,
    Wi' nod a gradely shelterin' place to rest.

G

A'wd try to write o' summat verra funny,
  Bud everything aw see seems lapped i' crape ;
Peas, an' poets, flourish when its sunny,
  When th' weather mends aw's happen ged i' shape.

Aw would so like to write o' glorious summer,
  Of o them beauties pictured in its skies ;
O'th' busy bee an' mony a merry hummer,
  Bud if aw do aw's hev to write sum lies.

A'stid o' fans, o th' women hes umbrellas ;
  Neaw if ther's summer here id does'nd show ;
If almanac's an' sitch like dud'nd tell us,
  Ther's nowt i' Blegburn here would ever know.

An June ull soon hev left us o together,
  An nod a smell aw've hed o' new med hay ;
What's good o' Summer comin' beawt her weather,
  Aw've nod a hauf a chance to ged away.

Aw connod feel a poet's sweet emotion,
  To tell yo' th' truth aw'm geddin gradely curled ;
When Summer looks so shabby it's a caution,
  It's nod like this i' other perts o'th' world.

If th' sun would nobbut show as id wer day time,
  If th' sky worn'd hanging deawn so low and dark ;
Bud dash id o ! ther's beawn to be no haytime,
  An o' these Irish labourers eawt o' werk !

Ther'll nobody like thee, Summer, nobbut th' cabby,
    He knows ther's fooak hooafe dreawn'd i' every street ;
Aw never thowt o' seein' thee so shabby,
    Look heaw thad dress o' thine's bin drabbled i'th' weet.

Aw's hev to stop, aw corn'd write whol its leeter ;
    Aw find this week my seet hes wossend fast ;
Let's dry eawr tears an' mek eawrsels look breeter,
    An' mek amends for th' gloomy looks o' th' past.

                    June, 1890.

Ribchester Club Walk.

A chap is a slave when he's lazy,
    He's a verra herd mayster to serve ;
Owd sloth is a thief an' a tyrant,
    As steyles o eawr pleasures an' nerve.
This week he's hed me in his clutches,
    Bud neaw, like a Briton, aw'm free ;
An' serve him as will, he's a bad 'un,
    Ther's nowt abeawt him as suits me.

Wi' kearin' i' th' nook aw wer gaumless,
    An' th' storin' to me wer a pain ;
To tek mo off feelin' so lazy,
    Aw seet off a trampin' i' th' rain.

Aw knew id wer Ribchester club walk ;
   Aw knew, too, they'd be i' ther glee ;
Aw'm awlus so fain when aw see 'um,
   An' sum on 'um's fain to see me.

Bud eh ! whod a long while aw loiter'd,
   For th' rooases wer smellin' so sweet ;
Mi heart aw could feel id go faster,
   As nearer th' owd city aw geet ;
For th' band seawnded sweetly i' t' distance,
   An' th' church bells wer ringin' a peal ;
Whenever aw gooa to th' owd city,
   My pen ull nod write whod aw feel.

Bud eh ! aw wor sorry for th' childer,
   They cried because th' day wer so weet :
Then smiled through ther tears at ther pennies,
   An' run off to spend 'um up th' street.
Neaw though aw'm so fond o' breet sunshine
   As leets up th' derk corners o' th' land,
It's nowt if id worn'd for th' breet faces,
   An' th' grip when aw tek a friend's hand.

June, 1890.

LIST OF SUBSCRIBERS.

Abbot, Percy, Blackburn.
Ainsworth, Wm., Pleasington.
Almond, John, Blackburn.
Alston, Albert, Burnley.
Alston, James, Ribchester.
Anderton, Edward   ,,
Arthur, George, Blackburn.
Arthur, W. D.   ,,
Ashton, Wm. T , Esq., J.P.,
    Darwen.
Ashworth, Thos , Blackburn
Aspden, Martin   ,,
Aspden, Martin   ,,
Aspden, Thos. A , Esq., J P.,
    Balderstone.

Balderstone, Ed , Padiham.
Ballard, William,   Blackburn.
Bannister, Miss A.   ,,
Bannister, Miss A.   ,,
Bannister, Wm. Hy., C.M. ,,
Baron, J. T.   ,,
Baron, Joseph   ,,
Baron, Wm.   ,,
Barton, Richard, Ribchester.
Barton, Rd.   ,,
Barton, Rd., junr.   ,,
Barton, Wm., junr.   ,,
Bass, John, Blackburn.
Bates, Jno. Dalton, Halifax.
Bayliss, Ed., Padiham.
Bebbington, J. C., Manchester.
Bebbington, J. C.,   ,,
Bennett, Joe, Longridge.
Bennett, John Wm., Ribchester.

Bennett, William, Ribchester.
Billington, Joseph, Blackburn.
Bilsborough, A.   ,,
Binns. R., Douglas.
Blackburn, Sarah A., Blackburn.
Bolton, Joseph   ,,
Bolton, Martin   ,,
Booth, Thos., Ribchester.
Booth, Thos.   ,,
Boyle, Wm., Blackburn.
Brandwood, Thos. ,,
Bransby, James, Southport.
Breakall, Thos., Blackburn.
Brooks, Jonathan, Barrow.
Brown, Barter, Ribchester.
Brown, J. H., Salford.
Bullock, Joseph, Padiham.
Burgess, Thos. L., Blackburn.
Butterfield, Wm.   ,,
Butterfield, Wm.   ,,

Calderbank, Wm., Blackburn.
Callendar, Wm., senr., Ribchester.
Callendar, Wm., junr.   ,,
Callis, Marmaduke, Blackburn.
Calvert, Rd.   ,,
Chew, Henry   ,,
Clark, William   ,,
Clarkson, Bartle, Ribchester.
Clarkson, Wm.   ,,
Cocker, James, Padiham.
Coddington, Wm , Esq , M.P.,
    Blackburn.
Coddington, Wm., Esq., M.P.,
    Blackburn.

Colman, Patrick, Padiham.
Corderley, Robt., Royton.
Corless, William, Blackburn.
Coupe, John   ,,
Counsell, Wm.   ,.
Coward, W. J.   ,,
Cowley, J. T., Manchester.
Cronshaw. John, Blackburn.
Crook, John   ,,
Crossland, Ralph   ,,
Crossley, R. S., Accrington.
Cunliffe, Wm. Hy., Blackburn.

Davies, Edward, Padiham.
Dawes, William, Blackburn.
Dewhurst, Edmund, Ribchester.
Dewhurst, Thos.   ,,
Dewhurst, Wm.   ,,
Dolpin, Wm.   ,,
Draper, J. M.,   Blackburn.
Dunbar, R.P., M.D.   ,,
Dunbar, R.P., M P.   ,,
Duncan and Mills, Bolton.
Duncan, John H.   ,,
Dunn, Matthew, Blackburn.
Dyson, Thomas, Manchester.

Eccles, George, Ribchester.
Eccles, Lawrence, Blackburn.
Eccles, Thos., Preston.
Eddington. Wm., Nelson.
Eddleston, Wm., Blackburn.
Eddleston, Wm.,   ,,

Fielden, Alfred, Blackburn.
Fielden, James   ,,
Fish, John, Livesey.
Fletcher, John, Ribchester.
Forrest. Thos., Blackburn.
Free Library   ,,
Free Library   ,,
Free Library, Clitheroe.

Galloway, Rd., Pleasington.
Garsden, James, Blackburn.
Garstang, W., M.D., M.R.C.P.,
    Lon., etc.,   Blackburn.
Graham, Joseph,   Blackburn.
Graham, Margaret   ,,

Green, Councillor G.   ,,
Greenhalgh, J. H., J.P., Bolton.
Greenhalgh, W. A.   ,,
Greenwood, Wm., Blackburn.
Grime. John, M.D.   ,,
Grimshaw, Miss   ,,
Grosart, A. B., D.D., L.L.D.,
    F.S.A.,   Blackburn.

Hacking. Geo.   ,,
Halliwell, M.   ,,
Halliwell, M.   ,,
Hanrahan, Rev. J.   ,,
Hargreaves, J., Padiham.
Hargreaves, John, Blackburn.
Harrell, Thos.   ,,
Hartley, James   ,,
Hartley. Wm.   ,,
Haydock. Wm.   ,,
Hayhurst, Wm. Hy.   ,,
Haythornthwaite,Wm.,Cherry Tree
Haythornthwaite, Wm.   ,,
Haythornthwaite, Wm.   ,,
Haythornthwaite, Wm.   ,,
Helm. Hargreaves, Padiham.
Helm, Richard   ,,
Hesmondhalgh, John, Ribchester.
Heyworth, Eli, Esq., J.P., Black-
    burn.
Higson, Henry, Blackburn.
Hindle, James   ,,
Hindle, John   ,,
Hindle, Robert, America.
Hirst, J. D., Blackburn.
Holden, Miss A.   ,,
Holden, Rd.   ,,
Holden, Wm.   ,,
Holmes, Hartley, Padiham.
Hornby, James, Blackburn.
Hothersall, Rd., Ribchester.
Hothersall, Wm.   ,,
Hoyle, Henry   ,,
Hughes, Peter, Padiham.
Hull, Geo., near Preston.
Hull, James, Blackburn.
Hull, William   ,,
Hulme, Wm.,   ,,
Hunt, Rothwell, Livesey.

Hunt, Rothwell, Livesey.

Ingham, Robert, Padiham
Ireland, Ann. Ribchester.
Ireland, John   ,,
Ireland, John   ,,
Ireland, John   ,,
Isherwood, Miss M., Padiham.

Jardine, John, Blackburn.
Jepson, Wm.   ,,
Jolley, John   ,,

Kay, Roger, near Ribchester.
Kendal, John, Blackburn.
Kenyon, J. H.   ,,
Kenyon, J. H.   ,,
Kenyon, Thos. Ribchester.
Kirwan, Rev. P. J., Mill Hill.
Kirwan, Rev. P. J.   ,,
Kirwan, Rev. P. J   ,,

Laycock, Samuel, Blackpool.
Lester, Joseph, Blackburn.
Livesey, Catherine, Padiham.
Livesey, Elizabeth   ,,
Livesey, Hannah   ,,
Livesey, James, Blackburn.
Livesey, Martha,   Padiham.
Livesey, Mary   ,,
Livesey, Matthew James ,,
Livesey, Mrs. E.   ,,
Livesey, Thos., Ribchester.
Livesey, Wm., senr., Padiham.
Livesey, Wm., junr.   ,,
Lonsdale, Wm. Hy., Blackburn
Lucas, Edward   ,,
Lucas, Thomas   ,,
Lucas, Wm. J.   ,,
Lucas, Wm. J.   ,,
Lucas, Wm. J.   ,,
Lund, Lemartine, Padiham.

McNally, Chas., junr., Padiham.
McQuaid, John, Blackburn.
Margerson, Luke,   ,,
Martin, John, M.H., M.D.,
     F.R.C.S., Blackburn.

Martin Thos., Ribchester.
Marwood, Councillor F., Pleasing-
     ton
Mather, Gilbert Blackburn.
Meadows, Mrs. J.   ,,
Mechanics' Institution, Bacup.
Miller, W., Bolton.
Moore, Thos., Blackburn.
Moorhouse, Theo., Padiham.
Morris, John T., Blackburn.
Moss, Wm. Robt.   ,,
Mullineaux, Alice A., Ribchester.
Mullineaux, John W.   ,,
Mullineaux, Mary A.   ,,
Mullineaux, Matthew   ,,
Mullineaux, Rd.   ,,

Naylor, Walter, Bolton.
Neville, John, Blackburn.
Neville, John   ,,
Neville, Thos.   ,,
Newton, Rev. Hy, Ribchester.
Newton, Rev. Hy.   ,,
Nichol, John, Rochdale.

O'Neill, John, Blackburn.
Ormerod, Edward ,,
Oxley, Thos., Padiham.

Parkinson, James, Blackburn.
Parkinson, Mrs C.   ,,
Patchett, J., L R.C.P., L.F.P.S.G,
     Great Harwood.
Patchett, J, L.R.C.P., L.F.P S.G.,
     Great Harwood.
Pearce, Rueben, Halifax.
Pearce, Rueben   ,,
Pearce, Reuben   ,,
Pearson, Joseph, Salford.
Pickering, Miss E.,   Blackburn.
Pickop, John, Esq, J.P. ,,
Pickup, George   ,,
Pickup, James   ,,
Pickup, John   ,,
Pinder, James, Ribchester.
Pinder, John, Blackburn.
Pinder, Richard, Padiham.
Pomfret Thos. Hy., Blackburn.
Powell, A., Bolton,

Pye, Thomas, Padiham.

Rawcliffe, Elizabeth, Blackburn.
Rawcliffe, Ellenor   ,,
Rawcliffe, Ellenor   ,,
Rawcliffe, John, Nelson.
Rawcliffe, Joseph, Blackburn.
Rawcliffe, Martha   ,,
Rawcliffe, Miss, Wiswell, near Whalley.
Rawcliffe, Mrs. E., Blackburn.
Rawcliffe, Richard   ,,
Rawcliffe, Thos., senr. ,,
Rawcliffe, Thos., junr. ,,
Riley, John, Padiham.
Robinson, Wm. H., M.R.C.S., L.R.C.P , Blackburn.

Sagar, John, Padiham.
Salisbury, Ed., Blackburn
Salisbury, John, Ribchester.
Sayer, Wm., Blackburn.   ·
Schofield, John ,,
Seed, Hugh, Bolton.
Sharples, Edgar, Great Harwood.
Sharples Edgar   ·   ,,
Simpson, G. D., Bolton.
Simpson, G. D   ,,
Simpson, G. D.   ,,
Simpson, Wm., Ribchester.
Slingsby A , Blackburn.
Smith, John   ,,
Smith, John   ,,
Southworth, James, Ribchester.
Southworth, Joseph, Blackburn.
Southworth, Margaret   ,,
Standing, Geo.   ,,
Stothert, T.   ,,
Sutton, C. W., Free Library, Manchester
Swindlehurst, Mrs., Blackburn.
Swindlehurst R. H., Mem. Inst. C.E., Bolton.

Taylor, R., Rochdale.
Taylor, Wm , Bolton.
Taylor, Wm.   ,,
Taylor, W. J. G., Withington.
Tennant, Geo., Mill Hill.

Threlfall, H.,   Blackburn.
Thompson, James   ,,
Thompson, Richard, Padiham.
Thompson, W. H., Blackburn
Till, Joseph   ,,
Tomlinson, Chas.   ,,
Toulmin, Geo.   ,,
Toulmin, John   ,,
Turner, James   ,,

Wade, John Thos., Padiham.
Walkden, Ellenor, Blackburn.
Walkden, James   ,,
Walker, Gregory   ,,
Walker, John, Warrington.
Warburton, Geo., Blackburn.
Warburton, Rd.   ,,
Ward, Miss Jane A., Blackburn.
Waring, John   ,,
Walmsley, Hugh, Padiham.
Walmsley, John, Blackburn.
Walsh, James Nelson.
Walton, James, Wakefield.
Walton, John, Ribchester.
Walton, Joseph   ,,
Walton, Wm., Wakefield.
Wells, Wm., Blackburn.
Welsby, Thos   ,,
Westwell, Thos.,   Padiham
Whalley, Robt. West ,,
Whewell, Thos., Blackburn
Whiteside, Miss E., Ribchester.
Whittaker, Henry, Blackburn.
Wilkinson, Ed   ,,
Wilkinson, Hy   ,,
Wilkinson Matthew Padiham.
Wilkinson, Wm., Ribchester.
Wilkinson, W. K., M.A., B'burn.
Wilson Dr. Robt.   ,,
Wilson, G. A., L.R.C.P.   ,,
Wilson, Miss E., Ribchester.
Wingham, Thos., Padiham.
Wise, William, Manchester.
Witton, James, Blackburn.
Wood, Edward, Blackburn.
Wood Henry   ,,
Wood James   ,,

Yates, Henry   ,,